W9-CCU-029

GREAT DETECTIVES

GREAT DETECTIVES

SEVEN ORIGINAL INVESTIGATIONS

JULIAN SYMONS

ILLUSTRATED BY

TOM ADAMS

HARRY N. ABRAMS, INC., PUBLISHERS, NEW YORK

Published in 1981 by Harry N. Abrams, Incorporated, New York

Library of Congress Cataloging in Publication Data
Symons, Julian, 1912–
Great Detectives.

1. Detective and mystery stories, English.
I. Title.
PR6037.Y5G7 1981 823′.912 80-28444
ISBN 0-8109-0978-2

Typeset in Linotron
11 on 13pt Horley Old Style by Tradepools Limited, Frome, Somerset

Illustrations originated on a Magnascan 460
by Barrett Berkeley, London

Printed and bound in Italy.

CONTENTS

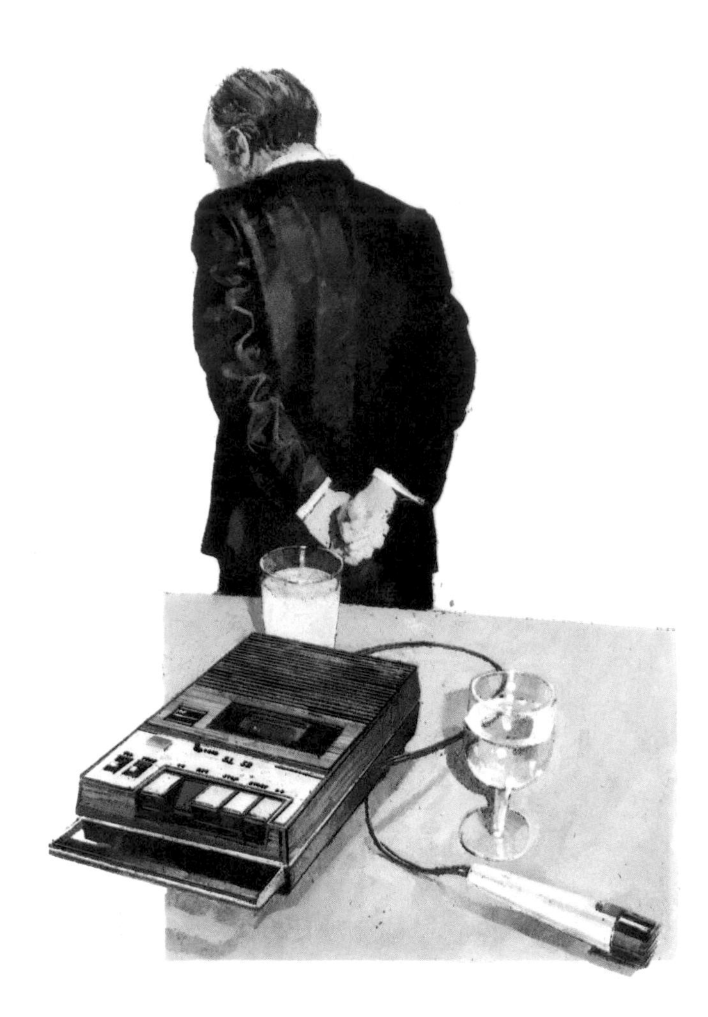

INTRODUCTION

THE GREAT DETECTIVES ARE CREATURES OF myth, and deserve the capital letters I have given them. They belong to the world of Don Quixote and Sancho Panza, or that of King Arthur and the Round Table, and are not to be circumscribed by dates or trapped in the silken web of fact. When I was invited to write their biographies my first reaction was to say that the task was impossible, that we had too much information about some of them, and too little about others, for them to be written about in biographical terms. My next was to reflect that if some of the 'facts' given us by their creators were blended with inventions of my own, the result might be entertaining to read. Supposing, further, that I introduced myself into some of the pieces as an enquiring biographer, they could also be amusing to write. The technique would need to vary from one detective to another, the story should suggest the master without ever attempting to enter into competition with him, parody must be avoided, and although this was planned as an illustrated book the text must have its separate interest, even without the pictures.

Those were the thoughts with which I began, and I hope they have been fulfilled. The Sherlock Holmes story relies very little upon biographical detail, chiefly because there is no shortage of biographies and biographical essays in the form of full-length books, which may easily be consulted. What is offered here is Sherlock in retirement, and a narrative which has a tease, if not exactly a twist, in the tail. In the case of Miss Marple (the only woman distinguished enough to be admitted into this gallery) it seemed a pleasant idea that the story of her life – of which the details, to be truthful, are scanty – should be told by the Vicar of St Mary Mead, who recounted the very first full-length Miss Marple story to be published.

The writer as biographer appears in the stories concerning Nero Wolfe, Ellery Queen and Philip Marlowe, and I hope he adds an individual flavour as well as providing variety. I certainly enjoyed my role as interviewer. At the same time, these pieces don't depend solely on my conversations with Archie Goodwin, Fred Dannay and a detective who is not Philip Marlowe. Aficionados of the noble Nero encounter him in what might be called Nero's Last Adventure, a surprising addition to the Queen family is discovered in the story about Ellery, and the links between Raymond Chandler and his detective are shown to be even closer than might have been suspected.

Maigret presented a similar problem to Sherlock Holmes. Simenon has written in such detail about his detective, and Maigret's own memoirs are so full and so informative, that it seemed pointless to repeat what had already been better said. I have tried to catch something of the abrupt, casual Simenon tone, and have sketched a minor Maigret adventure, with a glimpse of him at home with Madame Maigret. And finally, in the case of Hercule Poirot, there is a fairly straight biography, given in part to showing that Poirot was not a centenarian when he died. It is true that this biography also has an unusual feature, since it is based on the notes of Captain Hastings.

In taking such liberties with these Great Detectives I asked for, and obtained, the consent of their creators or descendants. Georges Simenon granted permission readily, and Frederic Dannay responded with characteristic warmth and generosity in relation to Ellery Queen, even contributing the name of one character. I am grateful to them both, and also to Helga Greene, Rosalind Hicks and estate of Rex Stout, for their kindness in allowing me to print these pastiches. And my warmest thanks go to Alison Cathie, a paragon among editors, and her assistant Kate Strachan.

I must say something about what will be for many the most exciting and controversial part of the book, Tom Adams's illustrations. They have such a beautiful fidelity to period feeling, and conform so closely even in minor details to the stories, that I exclaimed with pleasure at their style and subtlety. Maigret's office (his new one) is as Tom and I saw it in the Quai des Orfèvres by permission of the Paris police, something like the boucherie chevaline may be seen in the Rue de Seine, in the Marlowe story Nosy O'Donnell and Lefty Hansen are just right, and the final shoot-out catches perfectly the style of the thirties and adds subtlety to it by the splendid period chair and table, and the delicacy of the colouring. And I am sure that Nero's orchid room, Sherlock's cottage, the pictures of Ellery and his father, will give as much pleasure to others as they have done to me.

The word *controversial* comes into play in relation to the depiction of the Great Detectives. Most of them remain unpictured in books, and have been shown only by grotesquely inaccurate figures on stage and screen. Margaret Rutherford and Charles Laughton were splendid actors, but they looked ludicrously unlike Miss Marple and Poirot as described on the page.

It is partly because of this that readers have an image of these Great Detectives in their heads, and one is tempted to think that every reader has a different image. We all think we know what they look like, and the way an artist shows them will never conform exactly to the perfect picture in our mind's eye. To his devotees Nero Wolfe does not really look like a fat man even though he weighs three hundred pounds, Ellery Queen's accompaniment of pince-nez and walking stick must not make him appear foppish, Poirot is not ridiculous in spite of his shortness, patent leather hair and shoes, and his habit of carrying his head to one side. The artist here has gallantly attempted the impossible, and has gone a long way towards squaring the circle.

It should be added finally that this work, in its small way, is unique. This is the first time that these Great Detectives have been brought together, in words and pictures, between the covers of a book.

Julian Symons April, 1981

ARTIST'S NOTE

I LITTLE DREAMT, WHEN REACTING WITH enthusiasm to Virgil Pomfret's original idea for *The Great Detectives*, what I was letting myself in for. It sounded like the most wonderful publishing idea since the Bible, a kind of criminal apocrypha, challenging and great fun. My euphoria lasted through the early stages, followed by a marvellous period of enthusiasm and hard work: reading, planning, researching, even a bit of location work in Paris! I had already known most but not all of these amazing characters. The gaps in my knowledge were filled in by Julian Symons's vast collection of crime fiction and of course by the master criminologist himself.

Then the 'biographies' began to arrive. I was struck by Julian's ingenuity and gradually became aware of the enormity of the task I had undertaken.

By great good fortune I was able to draw on the talents of two fellow artists to help me finish the task in time. In fact, without the skill and hard work of Roy Coombes and Ivan Lapper this book would never have seen the light of day. I am deeply grateful to both of them and to Paul Welti, art director extraordinary, who played a vital part in the creative process, along with his tireless assistant Sarah Reason. I would also like to thank John Longman and Christopher Parfitt for their able assistance.

On the whole it has been a labour of love, an enriching and nostalgic journey into other times and other places; I would have liked to have had more time to do justice to Julian Symons's text and to these great heroes. In spite of any shortcomings in my interpretations, they have become so much more real to me and, I hope, to you.

Tom Adams April, 1981

How a Hermit was Disturbed in his Retirement

The young woman who made her way up the track leading from the country lane in the direction of Beachy Head was tall and elegant, with fair hair just visible beneath a close-fitting hat, what is sometimes called a peaches-and-cream complexion, and innocent china-blue eyes. She wore a dress of a colour that was not quite cream, and sensible walking shoes. The grassy track with its hedge on either side was not steep, but it went upwards all the way, and when she reached the end of it she was breathing a little faster than usual, perhaps because of the climb, or perhaps from excitement.

At the end of the track, and not before, the cottage was visible. It stood by itself in a field, a small thatched cottage made of flint and ragstone, with leaded windows on either side of the front door. There were low hedges around the place, giving it a pleasant air of privacy, and she glimpsed a garden beyond a wicket gate. The air up here on the Sussex downs had a tonic freshness, and she breathed it in gratefully as she walked across the field. She was about to lift the latch of the gate when she was checked by a cry of 'Don't move! Watch out!'

She stood quite still, but turned her head. Some thirty yards away, on the other side of the cottage, a veiled, gloved figure was bending over a beehive. He seemed to be pushing something into a recess of the hive using, as she could see, extreme care. For two or three minutes he remained bent over the hive, then slowly straightened up and came towards her, lifting the veil and taking off the thick gloves as he did so.

'I beg your pardon for calling out so abruptly, but it is a ticklish moment when a new queen is introduced into the hive. There is a risk of rejection, and to avoid it I have developed a cage of a new type that can be slipped between two combs in the brood chamber—but I must beg your pardon again, for of course the introduction of a queen to the hive cannot be of such momentous interest to you as it is to me. You are the young lady from the *South Eastern Gazette*?'

She nodded. He removed the hat and veil, and she recognized the aquiline features and piercing eyes of Sherlock Holmes. He was very much as he had been depicted in the *Strand Magazine*, except that the years had grizzled his hair, and lines of age were graven in his cheeks.

He opened the door of the cottage, put away the bee-keeping apparatus carefully in a cupboard, and stood aside for her to enter. She looked round with a curiosity touched with awe. It was a comfortable room, but one that showed marks of a bachelor's untidiness. There were things that she recognized from descriptions in Dr Watson's accounts, the coal scuttle, which as she could see contained some pipes and no doubt also tobacco, the violin case, the piles of papers on a chest. On the wall were sporting prints — surely they must have come from Baker Street? Was that chair beside the fireplace the one in which the Doctor had sat so often?

Sherlock Holmes offered her that very chair, sat down opposite her, filled a pipe with very dark tobacco, and fixed upon her a gaze whose keenness made her a little uncomfortable. He took the letter she had written from some dozen lying on a table, and read it with care.

'I am at a loss to know how you found my address. Since my retirement I have done my best to conceal it, even to the extent of making public a totally inaccurate description of my little home.'

'I mentioned my aunt E – Evelyn in my letter. Dr W – Watson had been her physician and then became a family friend. He was kind enough to give my aunt your address.' She spoke with a slight, attractive hesitation.

'So it is my old friend Watson who has been careless — not for the first time, I may tell you — and it is to him that I owe your visit. I should tell you that the newspaper interviewer is one of the members of the human species that I most abominate. Their questions tend to the impertinent or the irrelevant, and the pieces they write are couched in slovenly English. Yet there was something that interested me in your letter, or I should not have replied to it. Fire away with your questions, which I shall answer only on the understanding that my little house is neither photographed nor in any other way identified, and that anything you write will be submitted to me for approval.' He glanced again at the letter, and settled back in his chair as she took a reporter's notebook and pencil from a capacious bag. She seemed almost at a loss how to begin.

'Do you live here alone?'

'Entirely alone, except for a woman from the village who comes three times a week to clean, tidy

up, and do some necessary washing and laundering. Otherwise I look after myself. My wants are few, simple food, and tobacco which I order by the pound. I grow my own vegetables, and keep my own hens at the back of the house. Once a week I go into Eastbourne, and I buy a batch of newspapers, although I rarely find anything to interest me in them. The world has moved on since the end of the Great War, for the most part in ways that I do not approve of nor understand. So I walk the downs in all weathers and keep my bees, who sometimes give me instruction in human behaviour. The industrious life of the worker bee, the installation of the queen who has no power, although the colony's life depends on her, the massacre of the drones when the late summer honeyflow is over — there are lessons to be read in the bee's existence, if the world's statesmen would learn them.'

Her pencil had been flying over the lines. 'The most recent collection of your cases, *His Last Bow*, was published a few years ago in 1917, and the last story was set in August 1914, the capture of the German spy Von Bork. Are there no l – later cases?'

Sherlock Holmes puffed at his pipe. Smoke rose and lost itself among the oak beams on the ceiling. 'There has been nothing since the Von Bork business. My world is not that of the motor car and the aeroplane. I am a skilful driver, but my chosen means of transport has always been the railway or the hansom cab.'

'So there will be no more records of your cases?'

'I do not say that. I am out of touch with Watson, but I have given him permission to record what stories he wishes, and have even made notes myself about a couple of matters. Watson does not always choose the cases that seem to me most interesting — I always wished that he'd written about the problem of James Phillimore's disappearance — but Watson makes his own choice. I daresay he may put together another collection in his own time, but they will all be cases from the past.' He paused. 'But I am sorry to say that my old friend has taken to the bottle recently and is frequently in a state of stupor, so that there is little likelihood of his putting a book together.'

'And you undertake n – no cases at all now?'

Holmes put down his pipe, leaned over and took the pencil from her fingers. 'Let us stop this nonsense. You do not work for the *South Eastern Gazette* or for any other paper. Tell me why you came to see me, and what it is that has agitated you so much.'

'I – I – was it so obvious that I am not a newspaper reporter?'

'To me, very obvious. Your letter was written by hand, on paper with a private address. A genuine reporter would have used the newspaper's headed stationery, and most probably a typewriter. On one of my visits to Eastbourne I telephoned the editor of the *South Eastern Gazette* and learned that nobody with your name was on the staff. It was then that I became curious about your object, and agreed to see you. When I watched you making notes, it became plain to me that you were using neither Pitman shorthand, nor the more modern Gregg, nor any other of the forty-seven kinds of abbreviated writing of which I may modestly claim to have made a study. You were putting down gibberish, nothing more. When, finally, I made a revelation about Watson, a revelation so shocking that it should have made you jump out of your chair — and one, I may say, in which there is not a word of truth — you paid so little attention that you merely went on to the next question you had prepared.'

'And my agitation? I hoped I had concealed it.'

'When a young lady, otherwise impeccably dressed, comes here wearing odd stockings — '

She looked down and blushed. 'Good Heavens!'

'The difference between them is very slight, a matter of the patterning around the seam, but now that skirts have gone up at least six inches above the ankle it is possible for the trained eye to notice such matters.'

'Mr Holmes, I wanted to see you to ask your help. I thought that you would pay no attention to a letter, but truly I am desperate. Please do not turn me away.'

'I should not think of doing so. Of what use are rules, if no exceptions are to be made to them? Now, put away your notebook. I shall make a pot of tea — retirement encourages the domestic virtues — and while we drink it and eat a slice of the bread I baked this morning, you may tell me your story.'

'It is my f – fiancé, C – Captain Rogers, Jack Rogers. He has disappeared. I fear that he may be dead.'

The tea had a delicate fragrance, the cups and plates were Spode, the thinly sliced bread was full of flavour. Sherlock Holmes said, 'I had noticed the ring.'

'Isn't it beautiful?' She slipped it off her finger and gave it to him. The stones sparkled as he held the ring up to the light and then, with a murmured excuse, looked at it through a glass which he took

How a Hermit was Disturbed in his Retirement

from a drawer before returning it.

'And now your story,' he said. 'The best place to start, usually, is at the beginning.'

As she told her tale she spoke more freely, and her slight stammer disappeared. 'I live with my parents, Mr Holmes. We are not a rich family, but I suppose we are quite well off. Our home is outside Guildford in Surrey, a house which is said to go back to Tudor times. I have no sister, but one brother, Bertie. He is — he can do foolish things, but I love him, we all love him. Bertie was very brave in the War and has found it hard to settle down since then. Now he is in a stockbroker's, but really the only thing he enjoys is driving about in his little Ford car.'

'And your father?'

She look startled. 'I beg your pardon?'

'What is your father's occupation?'

'Oh, papa has no occupation in that way, he has no connection with business and I suppose he is awfully unbusinesslike. He goes into Guildford three days a week to the bridge club — I believe he is one of the finest players in the country — and then he is secretary of the local topographical society and president of the cricket club. All of those things take up time. Papa sometimes says he wishes there were more than twenty-four hours in the day, there is so much to do.'

'I can see that might be so,' Holmes said drily. 'And I assume that you are not in employment?'

'No. Papa sent me to a convent school. Our family has religious connections — one of my uncles is a canon of Chichester Cathedral. I have always thought that I should like to do something — something useful, like — oh, like nursing lepers. But papa and mamma were against it. I should like to have a job, there are times when I wish I truly was a reporter, but I know that papa would not think it a proper occupation for a lady. He has agreed that I should train to be a concert pianist, and I go up to London twice a week to a music school. Papa and mamma say I play beautifully but truly, Mr Holmes, I do not think I have the talent.'

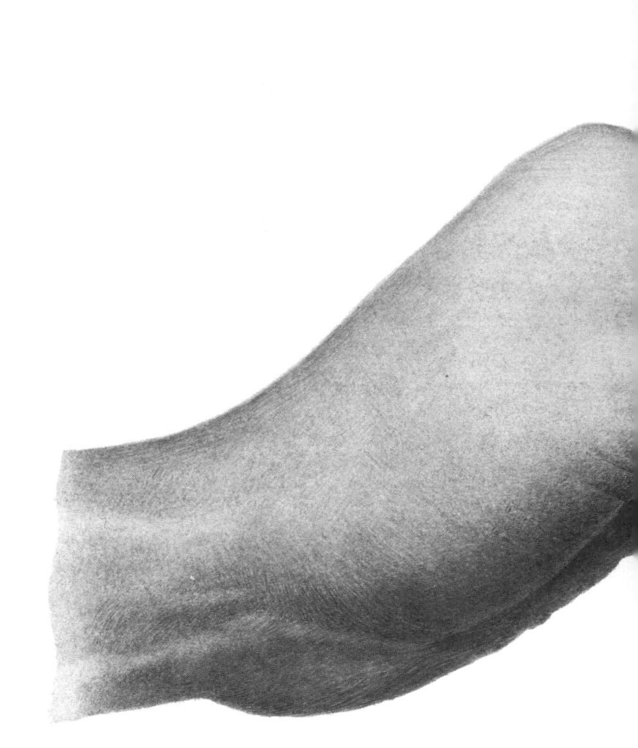

'Was it in connection with the music school that you met Captain Rogers?'

'Oh no, that was through Bertie. Bertie has very convenient rooms in the West End — I think papa helps to pay for the rent — and there is a small spare bedroom where I sometimes stay. One evening Jack, Captain Rogers, came round for a drink, and I met him. Shortly after that he asked me out to dinner, then to a dance, and I took him down to meet papa and mamma. They liked him, nobody could help liking him. And we became engaged. Here is a photograph of Jack, taken in the garden at home. He is laughing, you see, Jack is always laughing.'

Holmes studied the photograph, which showed a tall, dark young man. A cap was perched on his head at a rakish angle, and he was indeed laughing. 'He is much older than you.'

'Ten years older, but I like that. I think a husband should always be older than his wife, so that she can look up to him and respect him.'

'I suppose Captain Rogers is an old friend of

your brother? Perhaps they knew each other in the War?'

'Oh no, Bertie and Jack had known each other only a few days, and they couldn't have met in the War because Bertie was in France, and Jack was out in Palestine first of all and after that, well, he won't tell me exactly what he did, but I understood from Bertie it was awfully hush-hush.' She evidently gathered her courage for the next question, fingering the amber beads she wore round her neck. 'Mr Holmes, I have heard it said that during the War, after your capture of Von Bork, you were engaged on other work for our Secret Service. Is that true?'

A slight smile curved the detective's thin lips. 'You are even more innocent than you appear if you expect me to answer such a question.'

She flushed, 'I do not mean to be impertinent, but I thought that Jack might have been one of your colleagues, and that you would then have recognized him.'

He shook his head. 'I can assure you that, whatever I may have done in those years, it had no connection with your fiancé. But please continue your story. I take it that your parents not only liked Captain Rogers, but approved of him as your future husband.'

'Yes. Papa and mamma only want me to be happy, and I am — I was — wonderfully happy. And then Bertie is always singing Jack's praises, saying he's a go-ahead fellow and a good sport, and has all sorts of ripping ideas for making money. He hasn't got any, you know. Money, I mean. There was a sort of family conference when Jack said he wanted to marry me, papa and mamma and Bertie and me, and Jack told us about his father being an unsuccessful inventor who always hoped to make a fortune and never did. Both his parents were dead by the time he was eighteen, so that he had to make his own way in the world. Then he said: "I want to marry Jane, sir, but I must be frank and say I haven't a penny of capital to bless myself with, and I can't blame you if you turn me down." I knew what papa would say to that. He replied that if we loved each other, that was all the fortune we should need.'

'I see. Was nothing said about the way in which you would live, how your husband would support you?'

'Indeed, that was discussed. Papa said that it would be a sad thing if he could not help his only daughter to a happy start in her married life. Jack *hates* London, he wants to settle in the country and believes there is a fortune to be made by new methods of farming — oh, he has all sorts of interesting ideas, Mr Holmes, I wish you could hear him explain them. At the end of our conference papa agreed that if we found a house we liked, and that had some good farming land with it, he would buy it for us and provide the capital to give us a start. I know what you must be thinking, Mr Holmes, that it sounds like fortune-hunting, but if you met Jack you would not think that, he cares so little about money.

'So it was settled, and we began to look for houses. Jack knew I should not want to be far away from my family, so we looked in Surrey and Sussex.

Those were happy days for me, we would set out each morning in Jack's Overland tourer and look at houses. Jack knew at once whether a place was suitable. No, no, he would say, this is too dark, even your bright eyes won't light it up. Or the approach was too awkward, or the outbuildings hopeless, or the ground unsuitable for the crops he wanted to grow. Then after a week we found Hillerman Hall, a mile or two into the country from Reigate, and Jack said at once that this was the place. Mr and Mrs Pringle had been farming there, but he had had a slight stroke and found the work too much for him. The Hall needs redecoration, and will be rather cold and draughty in winter, but Jack was in such ecstasies about the place that of course I said yes. Papa agreed the price with Mr Pringle, and the date of the wedding was fixed in August, three weeks from now.'

'Had you looked at other houses in the district?'

'We had seen two others nearby. I liked one very much, but Jack said that the ground was quite unsuitable.'

'One would have thought it would be similar to that at Hillerman Hall, but no matter. Please continue.'

'Mr Pringle moved to a house called Maple Lodge, at a little village near Beaconsfield. I thought we might have the redecoration done, and we saw a local builder and chose the papers, but Jack said we should not bother about it until we went off on our honeymoon, so that it would be all finished when we returned. He would meet me in London after my day at the school of music, and take me to the theatre or a concert, or we would go somewhere with Bertie. It was a busy time, because I was also ordering the wedding dress, and arranging all kinds of things for the wedding. Then, just two weeks ago to-day, Jack told me that he had to go away. I have not seen him since.'

'Tell me exactly what happened.'

'I am not likely to forget, Mr Holmes. We were in Bertie's little sitting room, although my brother was not there. Jack took my hands, and said, "Now, Jane, you must listen carefully. You know that during the War I was in secret Government service. I cannot give you details, but with this kind of work there is no such thing as retirement. One may be called on at any time, and that is what has happened. I must not tell you who has approached me or what I have been asked to do, but I have to leave to-night, and may not return for three or four days."

'You will be back for the wedding?'

'He had been serious, but now he threw back his head and laughed like the Jack I knew. "Oh, my lovely Jane, long before that. You'll hardly know I've been away."

'Is there danger in what you will be doing?'

'"No more than in crossing the road," he said, and laughed again. Then Bertie came in, and Jack kissed me goodbye, and I have not seen nor heard from him since.'

'Had he said anything more to your brother?'

'Yes. Bertie was reluctant to tell me, but eventually did so. It seems there had been a message from the Foreign Secretary himself, and Jack had been sent on a mission that would take him to either France or Germany. That was all Bertie knew. He said there was no need to worry, Jack could look after himself, but I fear that he is dead. If he were still alive, I am sure he would have found a way to tell me. Then I thought of you, Mr Holmes, and wrote that foolish letter. When I got here I did not dare to put my problem to you at once, I thought you would be so angry. And now, can you give me any hope?'

Holmes had been in a blue study. Now he roused himself. 'There are other houses near Hillerman Hall, are there not? And perhaps it is near the road?'

'Why, yes. It is quite near the road, and there are houses near. All the land is at the back. But what has that to do with Jack's disappearance?'

'Nothing, perhaps.' He rose. 'It is an interesting little problem, and one that should not be difficult to solve, although I greatly fear—' He checked himself. 'But I am theorizing without facts, the grossest of errors. Let me see. Give me fifteen minutes, and I am at your service.'

'But where are we going? To see Bertie in London?'

'I doubt if he could add anything to what he has told you. No, we must visit Mr and Mrs Pringle at their place of retirement in Buckinghamshire.'

In the train up to Victoria, and on the journey out to Beaconsfield, Sherlock Holmes refused to say another word about the case. He talked of music, saying that one of the few things he regretted in his voluntary retirement was the fact that he could no longer visit Covent Garden on a Wagner night or hear a concert at St James's Hall, nor could he drop in casually to one of the Bond Street picture galleries, 'although indeed I fear that the paintings shown in them reveal the aberrations of modern taste.' He spoke of various tales that were told about him in the district where he lived, that he was related to one of the Kings who had lost their thrones in the Great War, that he was a former monk who still preserved a vow of silence, and that he was a murderer who had been reprieved and released from prison. Then he spoke amusingly of Dr Watson, who was still in reasonable health, although too rheumaticky to venture far from home now, saying that Watson's infallible nose for the wrong solution was almost as valuable as an instinct for the right one. By the time they reached Beaconsfield, his companion found herself laughing at some of his stories, as she had felt that she would never laugh again.

Maple Lodge was a pleasant house on the outskirts of the village. Holmes had announced their forthcoming arrival by telegram, and Tom Pringle, a burly man with a firm handshake, greeted them warmly.

'It's an honour to have the famous Sherlock Holmes in our new home, although I understood you'd retired from practice. Is it something to do with the Hall that you wanted to know? And have you left Captain Rogers behind in London? Is it Mrs Rogers yet, may I ask?'

She blushed and shook her head. Holmes replied. 'One or two questions have arisen about Hillerman Hall, yes.'

'About farming the place, is it? We'd been there near on twenty years, and it's not the easiest place in the world to farm, what with most of the land being on a slope so that drainage is a problem. In the end it got too much for me after I had my stroke. Only a slight one, mind you, but Dr Thomas said, either you give it up or you'll be carried out feet first. But I thought Captain Rogers might have a few problems. He was a pleasant young fellow, but I don't reckon he knew much about farming.'

Jane's blue eyes were bewildered. 'But Jack has all sorts of new ideas. He said the land was perfect for what he had in mind.'

'Did he now, my dear? I wish him joy of it. But I don't see where you come in, Mr Sherlock Holmes.'

'It is a small problem relating to the past history of the house about which I have been consulted,' Holmes said smoothly. 'You say you were there nearly twenty years. There was no break in your occupation? No time when you left the place empty for a while?'

'Never. Running a farm is a full-time job. You don't take weekends off.'

'Nor holidays?'

'No holidays for farmers.'

Mrs Pringle had not spoken. Now she said timidly, 'There was that time, Tom, when we had the big storm and all the top floor ceilings came down.'

'Don't count that a holiday, do you? Had a new roof on, new ceilings, wallpaper, cost a fortune.'

'It wasn't a holiday, but we went away for two weeks while the work was done, don't you remember? And Mr Robinson looked after the place.'

'Bill Robinson from down the road,' Tom Pringle agreed. 'Did his best I daresay, but a fine mess he made of it.'

Holmes leaned forward, his eyes gleaming. 'This was a time when you left the Hall unoccupied? Now, can you tell me the year and the month?'

The Pringles were agreed that the month had been June, and the year 1913. They were bewildered when Holmes said that he had nothing more to ask them, and so was Jane. She asked what all this could have to do with Jack's disappearance.

'It may be that I am on the wrong track, although the signs suggest otherwise. But now, my dear young lady, I propose to put you on a train to Guildford while I pursue my researches.'

She shook her head decisively. 'I shall stay with Bertie. I have already arranged to do so, and told papa and mamma. And Bertie knows that I have consulted you, indeed, it was his idea that I should pose as a journalist. I have the feeling that a communication from Jack might come to Bertie rather than my parents, if he needs help.' To this Holmes made no reply. With a flash of the spirit she had shown when pretending to be a journalist, she said, 'Since I seem to be cast in the role of Dr Watson, and you will not tell me your thoughts, may I at least ask where your research will take you?'

'If I say nothing, it is because I have ideas but no proof, so that they may be moonshine. You ask where I shall go to-morrow. I shall spend part of my time in the newspaper library of the British Museum, and the rest at Scotland Yard. The old hands have gone, Lestrade, Atherley Jones and Gregson, but Stanley Hopkins is still there, and he remembers me well enough to know that I never ask idle questions. Then the answers to those questions may take me further afield. As soon as I have news I shall send a telegram to your brother's rooms.'

The telegram was delivered late on the following evening. It said: 'Shall arrive early to-morrow. Then be ready for short journey. Sherlock Holmes.'

Holmes was as good as his word. It was no more

than a minute or two past eight when the bell rang. Bertie answered it, and ushered the detective in.

'Mr Holmes, you look tired. Would you like a whisky, or coffee and an egg? This is a bachelor flat, and my standards are not those of Mrs Hudson, but Jane and I will do our best.'

'Coffee and toast will suit me. I have been travelling much of the night, and age takes its toll.'

While Bertie made breakfast he came in and out of the room, and Holmes saw that the young man was remarkably like his sister, although there was a kind of wildness and irresponsibility about him, where she gave an impression of quiet strength. When they were at the breakfast table he said, 'Come on now, Mr Holmes, let's have it. What have you discovered?'

'The problem is solved, but the last act has still to be played. You are remarkably like your sister. I hope that you love her.'

'Why, I love Janie more than anybody in the world, she knows that.'

'I am glad to hear it. In the days ahead you may be able to comfort her, and undo some of the harm you caused when you introduced her to Jack Rogers.'

She clasped her hands tightly. 'Jack is dead. Is that what you are saying?'

'I almost wish I were saying that. You have been the victim of as cruel a trick as I remember. Laughing Jack Rogers — he has used other names, and sometimes calls himself Colonel or Commander as well as Captain — is one of the best-known confidence men in Britain. He specializes in making up to impressionable women and then robbing them of their savings. When necessary he goes through a marriage ceremony. Scotland Yard has a record on him as long as your arm, and it includes four bigamous marriages. Rogers came out of prison no more than three months ago.'

She put her head in her hands, but when she lifted it her face was composed, her eyes tearless. 'You could not have known this when I first told my story, Mr Holmes.'

'Of course not. What struck me immediately, however, was that yours is a much more than usually simple and credulous family. Here is a man known to none of you, who meets your brother casually, spins him a tale that cannot be checked about doing secret work in the War — work that no genuine agent would ever discuss — and is introduced to a young lady who knows very little indeed of the world and its wickedness. Your parents also are unworldly people, who believe every word the man says, and take it as a positive virtue when he tells them that he has no family and no capital. There is a whirlwind courtship, and he is accepted as a suitor.

'So the circumstances were suspicious. When I looked at the ring he had given you, and saw under the glass that the stones were not diamonds but almost worthless zircons, my doubts were strengthened. Of course if the fact had been noticed he would have said that he lacked the money to buy a diamond ring, and was ashamed to confess it. Was he simply a fortune-hunter? But as you told the story, it seemed that perhaps his object was not marriage, but had something to do with Hillerman Hall.'

'How do you make that out?' Bertie asked.

'Consider the position. He has been accepted, and the search for a suitable home is begun. Several houses are turned down, even though the prospective bride likes them. Hillerman Hall is seized upon, although she thinks it cold and draughty. The quality of the soil is said to be superlative, and yet it must be similar to that of nearby houses that have been rejected. And all this is seen to be nonsense when we learn from Mr Pringle that Rogers knows nothing about farming. Why then does he want the house? Why, when redecoration is suggested, does he say that it should be postponed until you are on your honeymoon?'

Holmes steepled his fingers and looked at them expectantly. 'You will forgive me for regarding this as an intellectual exercise, since seen in that light it has a certain fascination. When I asked myself that question *Why*, I could find no answer except that he wished to gain access to the Hall at a time when nobody else was there. It happens that I have been involved in two cases where an elaborate device was used to get somebody out of the premises they occupied. In the first instance it was to gain entrance to a cellar leading to a bank, in the other an attempt to recover a counterfeiter's outfit and his forged notes. I suspected that something of the same kind applied here, although the circumstances were different in the sense that the house was up for sale. When Rogers learned this he must have looked round for a dupe, somebody he could persuade to buy the place, perhaps in so-called partnership with him. He found you, and through you your sister. You need not reproach yourself too much. He is a most persuasive scoundrel.'

'That fits in with something Jack — Rogers — once said to me,' Bertie commented. 'He told me that he could make a fortune very quickly if he found a partner with some money. It was said in his usual joking way, and he soon saw that I had nothing. And then — I can never forgive myself for the sorrow I have brought on you, Jane.' She bowed her head again, in silence, as he placed his hand on hers. 'But are you saying that he had hidden something there?'

'If you will be good enough to follow my course of reasoning, I shall come to that in a moment.'

'But Mr Holmes,' said the irrepressible Bertie, 'forgive me for saying so, but shouldn't we set off now for Hillerman Hall?. We could go in Elsie, she'll take us there quicker than any train.'

'We shall do so all the more quickly, if you will permit me to finish,' the detective said with a touch of asperity. 'I ascertained from Jane that the house was near the road and had neighbours, so that if a thorough search of it had to be made, some caution must be observed. When we learned from the Pringles that the only time they had left the Hall was in 1913, I was confident that a search of the

HOW A HERMIT WAS DISTURBED IN HIS RETIREMENT

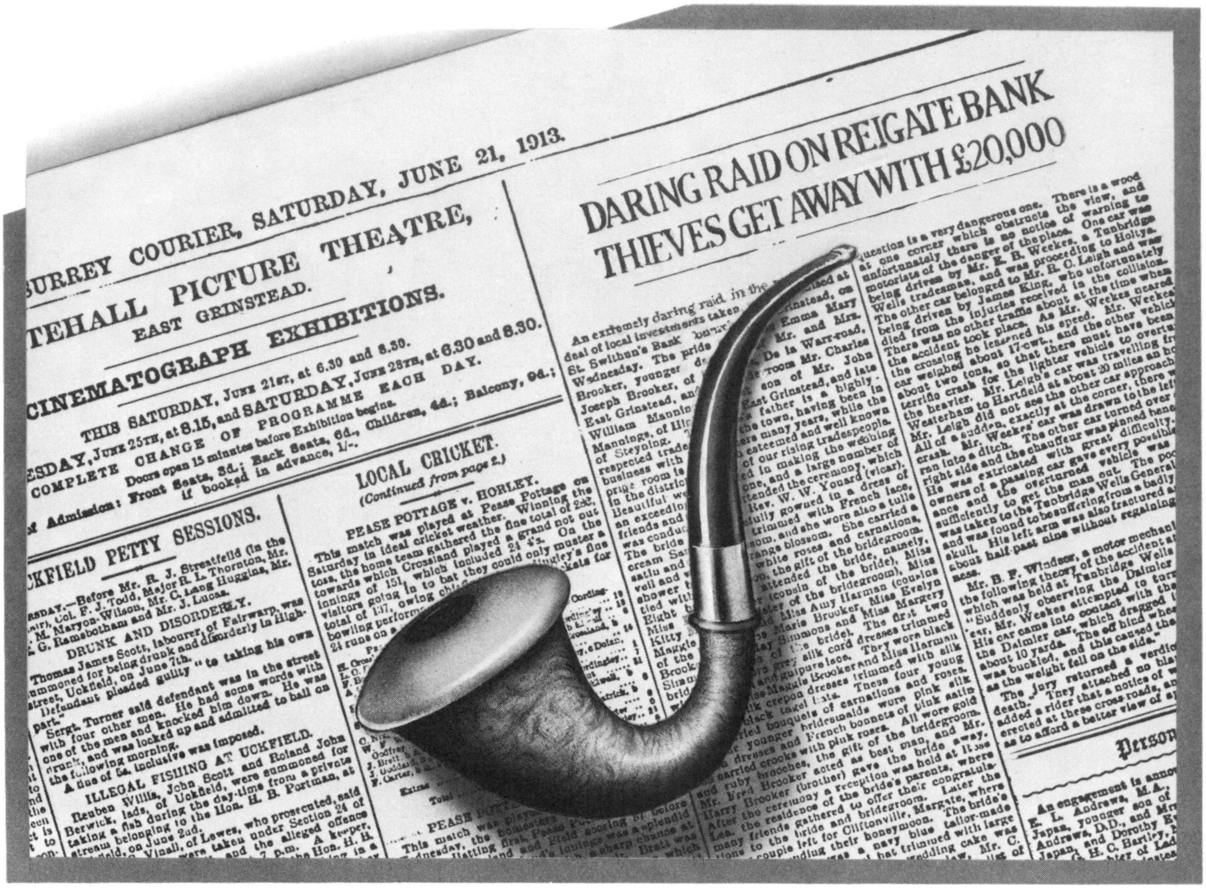

newspapers for that year would bring some answer to the problem of what had been hidden, and so it proved. In June 1913, a daring raid was carried out in the early evening on the Surrey and Sussex Bank at the Reigate branch. The thieves got away with more than twenty thousand pounds in notes, but they were interrupted by the assistant manager, who was beaten about the head and left for dead. He had raised the alarm, however, and the hunt was on. The thieves were caught at New Belton, which is no more than half a mile from Hillerman Hall. There were two of them, Black Ned Silverman and a man named Pascoe, and they got long sentences. Silverman had planned the raid, and got fourteen years. The money was never recovered.'

'So Rogers was not one of the gang,' Bertie said.

'No, he had nothing to do with it. Robbery with violence was not his game.'

'Then how did he know of it?'

'He was in prison with Black Ned, and for a time shared a cell with him. Silverman let slip something about the big job he had done, and said that the money was safely stashed away at Hillerman Hall. I said that Rogers is a persuasive devil.'

'If Rogers knows where the money is, surely he must have it by now.'

'I did not say he knew its location, Black Ned was not careless enough for that. We, however, have the advantage of him.'

Bertie stared open-mouthed. His sister, who had been listening attentively, said, 'Mr Holmes, you are a magician.'

'You flatter me. I have known Black Ned for a long time. Of course I disapprove his way of life, but he is not a bad fellow except for an uncontrollable temper. He trusts me, because I once got him freed on a charge of which he was not guilty. When I learned that he was involved I journeyed down to the Isle of Wight where he is serving his time. The Governor let me see him, and when I gave Black Ned the facts he told me what happened. When he and Pascoe saw that they were bound to be caught, they found this empty house, hid the money there and ran off so that they should not be caught on the spot. Pascoe died in prison, and Ned will not be out for some years yet, so he had little to lose by telling me where the money was located. He knew that Rogers would get it somehow if he was not caught. In any case, he wanted revenge. I should not like to be in Laughing Jack's shoes when Silverman comes out of prison.'

'He has had two weeks to look for the money,' Bertie said. 'How do you know that he has not found it and gone?'

Holmes smiled. 'Because I have been in touch with Inspector Beddoes of the local force, and learned that our man is still there. He works alone, as always, for Jack Rogers trusts nobody, and that limits what he can do each day. But there is an aspect of the affair which I think you do not appreciate, and which has brought me here to tell what I know must be a painful tale. Police action is not possible, for Rogers has committed no criminal offence. The house is one that he expects to occupy himself, and a man can hardly be charged with breaking into and damaging his own property. Once the engagement is broken it is a different matter. So that if you can bear to accompany me — '

The colour on Jane's cheeks was high. 'I should like to see him again. Once, just once.'

Bertie drove Elsie the little Ford with dash, hooting merrily as he passed other cars. At

Holmes's suggestion they stopped a few yards away and proceeded on foot. Hillerman Hall was gaunt and tall, a typical specimen of Victorian Gothic with something forbidding about its dull red brick. The entrance was a pointed archway, and above were steepled towers. As they approached they heard the sound of knocking, with something frantic, and even desperate about it.

The massive door opened when they turned the handle, and Jane exclaimed with astonishment as they entered. It looked as though a cyclone had gone through the large entrance hall. Floorboards had been ripped up and electric wires left trailing. A cupboard had been taken to pieces, half of the stairs banisters removed and the rail taken away and left on the floor. They went into a room on the right and saw the same trail of devastation. The knocking came from upstairs. Holmes put a finger to his lips and motioned to them to follow him. The sound came from one of the upper front rooms. The door of it was open, and the man inside had levered up some floorboards and was crouched low peering beneath them. A step-ladder stood in one corner.

'You are not likely to have any success there, Rogers,' Sherlock Holmes said. 'You should have wheedled Black Ned into giving you more details.'

The man sprang up with an oath, which was checked when he saw the other visitors. He was no less handsome than his photograph, but the laughing expression in the picture was replaced by a scowl, and then by a look of bewilderment.

'Bertie, Jane, what are you doing here? And who are you?'

'My name is Sherlock Holmes. I was called on by this young lady, because she feared for your safety. You told your tale too well.'

As though by magic, the vicious scowl and the bewilderment were wiped off Rogers's face, and replaced by a charming smile.

'Jane, my dear sweet innocent Jane—'

Her voice was like steel. 'I was innocent, I am so no longer. Is this your Government service?'

He laughed easily. 'Let me explain. You would have thought me ridiculous if I had told you that a fortune might be hidden in the house we had bought. I wanted to surprise you, to be able to say that I was not coming to you empty-handed after all.'

'No use, Rogers,' Holmes said harshly. 'They know the whole story.'

Again a change came over the handsome features, so that the smile was accompanied by a look of calculation. 'I have done nothing against the law.'

'So Mr James Windibank, alias Hosmer Angel, said on another occasion. I agreed, but threatened to thrash him with a horsewhip.'

'I can't say that I see a horsewhip to hand. And I must remind you that this house belongs to my future wife.'

He broke off, because she had removed the ring and thrown it at his feet. 'No longer. There is your worthless ring.'

'It cost a pound or two, but let it lie. And since our engagement is broken, perhaps after all it would be polite to relieve you of my presence.'

'Just a moment,' Sherlock Holmes said. 'You may like to see what you have been looking for so long.

When this house was empty it was in need of redecoration, and in particular the upper floor ceilings had come down. The workmen had finished for the day and left their equipment behind them. When Black Ned and Pascoe came in here, on the run, they knew they had not hours but only minutes to find a hiding place, and from what I was told they chose this very room.' Holmes was looking up at the ceiling. 'The ceiling was down, the laths exposed and a few of them loose. It was the work of five minutes to nail them back into place, after slipping the packages of notes above them. You should have thought of the ceilings, Rogers. The north-east corner, Black Ned said. This looks a likely area, where some cracks are showing.'

Holmes took the step-ladder across, got up on it and hacked away at the cracked place with a chisel until he brought down the plaster. Then, seeing nails that looked newer than the rest, he forced the chisel between them, put his hand in the space he had made, and brought it out holding a bunch of banknotes.

'There are more where these came from and, Bertie, I think your young arm would be well employed in extracting them. I should not be surprised if the Surrey and Sussex Bank made a handsome acknowledgment of their money being returned after all these years. As for you, Rogers, you are now a trespasser on these premises, and if you want to avoid trouble I should make yourself scarce. Your fiancée has had a lucky escape.'

The letter that came to Holmes's cottage a few days later was in a delicate and spidery, yet still characterful, hand. He read:

Dear Mr Holmes,

I do not know how to thank you. You said I knew nothing of the world's wickedness, but I have seen something of it now. Bertie is very ashamed of himself, saying that but for him I should never have become entangled with Jack. He thinks that he is not cut out for stockbroking, and may try his luck in the Colonies. Papa and mamma have been kind and consoling. We are an unworldly family, as you say, and they had never encountered a really bad man before. Neither had I.

As for myself, what can I say? I know the man I loved to be worthless, yet I shall never forget him. I am not sure whether there is any meaning in speaking of a broken heart, but I know that I shall never marry.

This does not lessen my gratitude to you. I shall always remain your devoted admirer. . .

'A trivial little case, with some points of interest, but hardly one for Watson,' Sherlock Holmes said to himself. He put the letter into the thin file containing the other relevant details. The young woman had impressed him by her strength of character as well as by her youthful innocence, and he indexed the case under 'M'. He could not quite read the surname: was it perhaps Mantle or Maple. . .?

MISS MARPLE'S HOME, 'DANEMEAD'

About Miss Marple and St Mary Mead

My name is Leonard Clement, and I was for many years Vicar of St Mary Mead. It was with some hesitation that I acceded to Mr Symons's suggestion that I should write something about the village and Miss Marple, but in the end my dear wife Griselda convinced me.

'After all, dear, you started the whole thing off,' she said. 'It is right that you should finish it. You know more about the village than anybody else in the place. And it will be something to occupy you now that you have retired.'

'There is one person who knows more than I do.'

'And who may that be?' she asked innocently.

'Why, Miss Marple, of course.'

We both knew, however, that Miss Marple would never be prevailed upon to write about herself. And although it was Griselda who persuaded me to write about Miss Marple, it is Mr Symons who suggested that readers would be interested to know something about the village. It is not, he pointed out, to be found on any Ordnance Survey Map.

That is true, and naturally there is a good reason for it. When I consented to write down that first story, it was on the understanding that the village should not be subjected to undesirable notoriety, and so I did not give its real name. The pseudonymity has been preserved ever since, although if I gave the true name readers would not be greatly enlightened. St Mary Mead is a perfectly ordinary pleasant English country village. Except, of course, that it has had more than its share of crime.

But I must not run on. First of all, let me describe St Mary Mead as it was. As the rough maps in that very first story suggested, there is really one road through the village, the High Street, although several lanes branch off it. Our railway station is on this main road, about a mile outside the village to the north west. The station is still in use, although there are not many trains, and they are all stopping ones. If you are coming down from London it is generally more convenient to get out at Much Benham, two miles away, and take Inch's taxi service, known to all and sundry as Inch. Our local paper is the *Much Benham Herald and Argus*, which has a column of St Mary Mead news each week. On the other side of the village the first place of any size is Market Basing, with the Hellingforth film studios nearby. Our nearest coastal resort, Danemouth, is no more than eighteen miles away. I suppose by giving these facts I may enable some painstaking investigator to identify the village precisely. However, nobody has done so yet.

That is the general setting. Coming into the village from the Much Benham road, you pass first of all some cottages, including the one occupied for a time by Lawrence Redding, and then on both sides there are shops. On the right you come to a cluster of Queen Anne and Georgian houses, the nicest in the village. There is Dr Haydock's house, which has its entrance down the lane, and next to that, rather further down the lane is the Vicarage, with its charming garden. Further down still is the home of Mrs Price Ridley, that large and dictatorial widow as somebody called her. The front entrance of Miss Marple's house 'Danemead' is on the village street, but the side of her garden runs down by the doctor's house and the Vicarage, so that when I was Vicar we were very near neighbours. Next to Miss Marple is gossipy Miss Hartnell, and next to her that perennial spinster Miss Wetherby, a mixture of vinegar and gush as I once called her. Their gardens all back on to another lane, from which a track runs down through woods to Old Hall, where Colonel Protheroe lived. Returning again to the High Street you come to the church on the left, and beyond it the 'Blue Boar'. Then, on left and right, there are the Village Hall, more shops like Barnes the grocer, Footit the butcher, our oddly named local chemist Cherubim, the local estate agents Biddle and Russell, and the basket shop run by Mr Toms. And the fishmonger, whose name I seem temporarily to have forgotten. Then yet another lane, on the left after the 'Blue Boar', leads to Gossington Hall rather more than a mile away, where Colonel and Mrs Bantry lived. And then the village peters out in a few more cottages, and the road leads on to Market Basing.

Such is St Mary Mead as it was, in the days when I rashly said that 'We are not used to mysteries in St Mary Mead.' Little I knew! And of course that was before Colonel Protheroe had been found dead at my writing table in the Vicarage study. What about the village as it is today? Some of the changes are the inevitable result of passing years. Dr Haydock, that fine strapping man with his honest boxer's face, has retired and been replaced by his partner Dr Sandford. A Dr Sims has what used to be called the panel patients. I have retired myself, and been replaced. I must express no doubt that this change is for the better. Miss Wetherby has passed on, and a bank manager now occupies her house. Mrs Price Ridley has gone to live at Cheltenham, and her house has had a variety of tenants. The fishmonger has smart new windows, and his fish is on refrigerated slabs. Mr Toms's basket shop has gone, replaced by a small supermarket. There have been additions to the Village Hall. Colonel Bantry is dead, and his wife has moved to the East Lodge at Gossington Hall. Most dramatic change of all is the Development, the new estate put up on the way to the Hall in which all the roads are called something-or-other Close, and the houses are full of well-turned-out young wives who shop at the supermarket because it is cheaper and easier. One of them came in every day to help Miss Marple, and she was a quick and efficient cook, although heavy-handed with the washing up.

So that is the village, and a few of its people. I hope I may be forgiven for some of the things I have said about them, and also for my words in the past about Griselda. A bad cook, incompetent in every way, extremely trying to live with, a very irritating woman—dear me, how can I have said

LEONARD AND GRISELDA CLEMENT

such things? And how can it be that Griselda preferred such a crotchety fellow to the baronet, company promoter, Cabinet Minister, and three subalterns, who all proposed marriage to her? Let me make what amends I can by saying that Griselda has become *a very good cook*, and that she has cared for and cosseted her tetchy old husband over the years. And I might add in my own defence that I said in the very first book how pretty Griselda was, and in my eyes she is still both pretty and youthful. It is true, of course, that she is nearly twenty years my junior.

And now, Miss Marple. Mr Symons has suggested that I should describe her origins, give an account of her house and habits, and say something about her attitude to life and people. I shall not deal with her achievements in solving many baffling crimes, because they have of course been covered in Mrs Christie's books.

I always understood Jane Marple's background to be vaguely clerical, although I never heard that her father had a direct connection with the church. She mentioned at various times that her uncle Thomas was a Canon of Ely, that another uncle was a Canon of Chichester Cathedral, and that she had gone to school for a time in a Cathedral Close. Her mother's name was Clara, but her father's is not known to me. About her childhood, she said that she had a sister and German governess, and I believe there was also a ne'er-do-well brother. She was taken to Madame Tussaud's as a child, had an early love affair which she did not describe in detail, and her father used to have his tea sent to his study when women were gossiping together — all I know of her early years is such fragments. She seemed to have no living relatives who visited her, except her nephew the novelist Raymond West, who I thought behaved very well to his aunt in view of the things she sometimes said about him and his wife Joan. I recall her remarking once that Joan West's art, which was highly regarded by well-known critics, consisted mostly of jugs of dying flowers, and broken combs on window-sills. She mentioned at one time a niece called Mabel, who was presumably

JOAN WEST

A FAMILY GROUP: MISS MARPLE, AUNT, UNCLE, SISTER

her sister's child, but I never knew the sister's married name, or where she lived. One cannot even be sure that Mabel *was* her niece, for she called Joan West by that name, although in fact she was only a niece by marriage. For that matter, she sometimes called Raymond West her great-nephew.

I often felt that some tragedy had marked her early life, although she never spoke of it. This may sound as though she was secretive, and it is true that she liked to keep herself to herself. If she did not wish you to know something, she had some masterly techniques for avoiding awkward questions while remaining polite. For example, Griselda was curious about her friendship with the two Martin girls, Ruth and Carrie-Louise. They met in a Florence *pensione* when Miss Marple was a 'pink and white girl from a Cathedral Close'. How had Miss Marple come to be visiting Florence on her own, Griselda wondered? But she never learned, for Miss Marple smiled her sweet smile, and began to talk about the coming Vicarage fête. We do know from Ruth van Rydock that when Miss Marple was young she thought of nursing lepers, but so far as I know she never carried out that intention.

She used sometimes to say that she had lived in St Mary Mead almost all her life, but that was far from true. If you read the accounts of her adventures, you will be surprised how much and how often she was away from the village — in the Caribbean and staying at Bertram's Hotel in London (thanks to the kindness of Raymond West), visiting a hydro, going to stay with old friends like Carrie-Louise Martin, going around here, there and everywhere. She let drop at one time that she had seen almost all of Somerset Maugham's plays, and she certainly did not see those in St Mary Mead. It sometimes seemed to me that she was hardly ever to be found at home.

And speaking of 'home', I must say something about her house. 'Danemead' was charming, one among the little nest of Queen Anne and Georgian houses that survived intact from the village's development. The way she kept it was a little finicky for my own taste or Griselda's, but I suppose accorded with her own personality, which was in many ways old-fashioned. The drawing room was small and crowded, although there were nice things in it. She had some fine Waterford glass, and an old Worcester tea-set which she removed from daily circulation when Cherry Baker went to work for her. Cherry was the young wife from the Development who came to help the old lady (as she called her) when Miss Marple was not quite able to look after herself. She annoyed Miss Marple by calling the drawing room the lounge, but to my surprise they got along for the most part very well. Cherry was intelligent and quick, and that pleased her mistress — although *mistress* is a word that Cherry, like many in her generation, would never have tolerated. She made it plain that she was just lending a hand to help out. Cherry was certainly very different from the other girls I knew who worked at 'Danemead', old-fashioned servants all of them. I can remember Amy, Clara, Alice, all from St Faith's Orphanage — or rather, Griselda has remembered the names, for I confess that in my mind they all blend into one pleasant girl wearing cap and uniform. They came for what was called training, and went on to better-paid jobs, for I know they were not paid a great deal at 'Danemead'. I remember an old grenadier named Florence, and Griselda says there was also a little maid called Evelyn. I think that is all.

THE WORCESTER TEA-SET

But, good Heavens, Griselda has reminded me that it is by no means all. There was also Gladys Martin, who was murdered, although not in the village. She came from St Faith's too, and was taught how to wait at table and keep the silver polished. What Miss Marple said about her after Gladys's death shows how sharp her tongue could be. Gladys, she said, had spots, adenoids, and was pathetically stupid. 'One doesn't really know what to do with the Gladyses.' But below that tart tongue was a Christian heart. As soon as she learned of Gladys's death, Miss Marple left St Mary Mead to investigate the case.

The garden at 'Danemead' was — well, Griselda once called it 'twee', which is not a word I would have used, but I know what she meant. Miss Marple was very good with roses, and was always looking for rarities to put in the rock garden. It was a black day for her when Dr Haydock forbade her to do any stooping or kneeling because they were bad for her heart, so that she was reduced to jobs like pruning. She took on part-time gardeners, a pensioner named Edwards, and then old Laycock. They were certainly not very good. 'Lots of cups of tea and so much pottering — not any real *work*', she said, and complained that they were so opinionated. Mind you, she could be opinionated herself.

That was the 'Danemead' household. I don't remember hearing that Miss Marple did any cooking, but she made cowslip wine and camomile tea. At one time she kept no drink in the house, but later on there was a little whisky in a corner cupboard. I don't think I ever went upstairs, but I was told that the dressing table legs were swathed in chintz. I should not be surprised if that were true, for she was in many ways a typical old maid. On the other hand, this was an image she cultivated.

She cultivated a certain image, too, in her appearance. She was tall and thin, with pink cheeks, deceptively innocent china-blue eyes and beautiful fluffy white hair, and even when dowdily dressed looked, as was said, every inch a lady. She struck most people as sweet, and even a little dithery. Here are one or two descriptions of her. 'The one with white fluffy hair and the knitting' (that was a policeman), 'a white-haired old lady with a gentle appealing manner . . . an elderly frail old lady', and so on. She may have looked frail, but when put to the test she showed great resilience and toughness. And she had some unsuspected skills. On one occasion she spoke in a dead woman's voice to unnerve a murderer, and we were told that she 'had always been able to mimic people's voices', although there is no other instance of her doing so. I have mentioned the word dowdy, but as Griselda has just said to me, I must not leave the impression that she was always or even often dowdy, far from it. There is a description of her at one of the Tuesday Club meetings, wearing 'a black brocade dress, very much pinched in around the waist' and with 'Mechlin lace arranged in a cascade down the front of the bodice'. With this she wore black mittens and a black lace cap, to complete the picture of an unworldly, out-of-date old lady. She was fond of lace. At another dinner party she had an old lace fichu draped round her shoulders, and a piece of lace on her white hair. Very becoming that looked, rather more so than the puce silk evening gown of which she was at one time extremely fond. As I have said, however, some of this was wear for special occasions, or was designed to convey an impression of being frail, and innocent of the world's wicked ways, an impression that was far from reality. I remember her best in good country tweeds, in which she always managed to look rather elegant. In winter she was much wound about with scarves.

THE GARDEN

I come now to the delicate matter of how Miss Marple was regarded in St Mary Mead. This is something about which Mrs Christie, not surprisingly, had almost nothing to say. I use the words 'not surprisingly', because the truth is that by many people she was not altogether trusted. Griselda's first reaction was to call her 'that terrible Miss Marple' and to say that she 'was the worst cat in the village . . . She always knows every single thing that happens — and draws the worst inferences from it.' Later on Griselda came to see that there was a lot of sugar mixed with Miss Marple's vinegar, but there is no doubt that she could have a sharp tongue. However, Miss Wetherby and Miss Hartnell (to name no others) could be sharp too. The real trouble was that crime seemed to follow Miss Marple, so that some people were afraid of having anything to do with her. First there was Colonel Protheroe's death, which I've already mentioned. Then there was the young woman's body found in Colonel Bantry's library up at Gossington Hall. There was the death of young Rose Emmott, daughter of the 'Blue Boar's' landlord. That would have been accepted as suicide by drowning if Miss Marple had not intervened, seen it was murder, and written down the murderer's name on a piece of paper. Very right and worthy, but some people said you should let the dead rest.

Then there was a great deal said about the later troubles up at Gossington Hall, after Colonel Bantry's death. That was quite a holocaust, four deaths, although the last was suicide. I have already mentioned the Tuesday Club, which met at Miss Marple's house to discuss unsolved mysteries. Sir Henry Clithering, who was formerly Assistant Commissioner at Scotland Yard, used to come along specially to those meetings. He called Miss Marple 'the finest detective God ever made — the super Pussy of all old Pussies'. That was all very well, and quite possibly he was right, but again people felt they didn't want the cleverest of old Pussies snooping about and spying (it was said) on everything they did.

It would be quite wrong, however, to convey the impression that Miss Marple had no friends. Griselda came to trust and love her, and I hope that I too may be counted as her friend. She was kind enough to say that in one case, the unhappy affair of the deaths among the film people at Gossington Hall, my memory helped her to solve the crimes. I

A MEETING OF THE TUESDAY CLUB

never quite understood what she meant, but was much gratified to have played a part in clearing up a mystery. But perhaps her greatest friends in the district were the Bantrys, who lived up at the Hall, which was very much the grandest house in the village. Not that the place was an architectural gem. 'Good, solidly built, rather ugly Victorian', somebody called it, and I shouldn't dissent from that. The Bantrys kept it up, as was customary in the old days, with a butler and what Mrs Christie once described as 'a knot of huddled servants'—huddled, of course, because they had just discovered a dead body in the library. But it was always a strain for the Bantrys to keep up the place properly, and after the Colonel's death Mrs Bantry, as I think I have mentioned, sold the Hall and moved into the East Lodge, which was pretty but inconvenient. Later on, when the film people got hold of the house, they put in several bathrooms and a number of incongruous picture windows, and knocked the study and library into one to make a music room. They also installed a swimming pool with lots of exotic shrubs around it. As Griselda said, they really *deserved* to have some murders there and I could not help agreeing with her, although of course I rebuked her for making such an unChristian remark. But anyway, Jane Marple was fond of Dolly Bantry. Indeed, I think she was fond of many of us, although she was too reserved to show her feelings openly.

And now I must address myself to the matter of assessing Miss Marple's attitude towards life and society. (Griselda, who has been reading and commenting on every page of this, says I have the gift of putting things in the most pompous and boring way. I replied that I could only put such things in *my* way, and that I hoped readers would forgive me.) I think that the thing which has struck me most strongly is her keen sense of evil so that, as she often said, she could sense it in the neighbourhood and almost smell it in the air. Going along with that was her intense interest in crime. I don't think that interest could be conveyed better than by her participation in the Tuesday Club, and her eager agreement that the meetings should be held at 'Danemead'. Sir Henry Clithering's presence at the meetings was natural enough, for he had a professional interest in the cases, and I was not surprised that the artist Joyce Lemprière was always present, for it does seem that crime is somehow linked with art. I suppose little dried-up Mr Petherick might also be said to have a professional interest since he was a solicitor, but quite frankly, when I learned that Dr Pender, a local clergyman, also attended the gatherings, I could not approve.

It says a lot about Miss Marple's personality that she could have been so much at the heart of the Club. And of course it says even more about her perceptiveness that she should have, as I understand, solved every one of the problems that baffled Sir Henry and the others. When he called her the finest detective God ever made, the last three words are important, for I think her gift came from God.

She said once that her mother and grandmother had told her that a true lady can neither be shocked nor surprised, and this certainly applied to her, although there were occasions when she showed indignation. One of these was when she was reading film magazines like *Movie News* and *Amongst the Stars* which specialized in 'confidential stories', and told nice young Inspector Craddock that she was shocked. What shocked her was not the stories themselves, but the scandalous way they were written. 'I'm rather old-fashioned, you know, and I feel that really shouldn't be allowed. It makes me sometimes very angry.' Another occasion when she showed strong feeling was when she learned that a clothes peg had been clipped to Gladys Martin's nose to conform with the nursery rhyme. That, she said, made her very angry. 'It was such a cruel, contemptuous gesture. It's very wicked, you know, to affront human dignity.'

I should add that those were exceptional occasions. For the most part she sat quietly with her knitting, or looking out of her window, noting all that was said and done—and, sometimes equally important, what was not said and not done. 'One so often looks at the wrong thing, though whether because one happens to do so or because you're meant to, it's very hard to say,' she said to a police Inspector, this time one named Curry, in another case. And sure enough, this was a case in which 'all the things that *seemed* to be true were only illusions,' and the villain had been playing a part throughout. It was characteristic of her to tease baffled Superintendents and Inspectors with village reminiscences, about the shifty eye of Fred Tyler at the fish shop which made it less surprising that he should slip an extra figure into the shillings column, or recalling an occasion in Paris when she had tea with her mother and grandmother, and her grandmother exclaimed that she was the only person there in a bonnet. And there were little village problems which she posed but never answered, like who cut the meshes of Mrs Jones's string bag, why Mrs Sims only wore her new fur coat once, and what happened to the shrimps Mrs Carruthers bought, which were missing when she got home. Almost always these anecdotes had a true relevance to the unfolded puzzle, although they could be fully understood only if you had a mind like Jane Marple's.

And what kind of mind was that? Why, one which was aware that a great deal of wickedness exists in the world, and that a microcosm of it may be found in an English village. I am a man of God, and I think that the truest phrase for Miss Marple would be that she was God's servant.

In Which Archie Goodwin Remembers

In his early thirties, from all the descriptions I had read, Archie Goodwin was attractive rather than handsome, a big, muscular six-footer with the light-coloured hair that is almost red, and regular features saved from being conventionally good-looking by the short broad-ridged nose which gave him an air of independence and slight cockiness. That had been a while ago, but although the hair was grey now he still gave the impression of physical power kept nicely under control to be expected of Nero Wolfe's close associate. The handshake was firm, the grey eyes gave me a searching, but not unfriendly look. There wasn't much those eyes failed to notice, and they took in now my rapid inspection of the room. There were things I'd read about in twenty books, but never seen. As I walked over to the big globe standing in one corner, he nodded approvingly.

'That's the three-foot globe that stood in one corner of the office, right.'

'It was a two-foot globe in the early days, or so I read.'

He said with a touch of sharpness, 'We didn't get around to measuring it. What else?'

'That red leather chair. Perhaps the sofa, although if so you've had it re-covered because it should be bright yellow. That petrified wood paperweight. Oh yes, and one or two of the engravings, like the one of Brillat-Savarin. And some of the books, I suppose, because I know you're not a great reader. At least, that's what you say, though I noticed that you knew what "apodictical" meant. I had to look it up in the dictionary.'

'Mr Wolfe used it and then I looked it up, thought I'd slip it into a story.' He grinned. 'Not bad, Mr Symons, you might make a detective.

You've missed the massaranduba table there in the corner, the perforated picture of Washington Monument over there which used to serve as a listening panel, and one or two other things. Still, not bad. Would you like a drink? Mr Wolfe used to keep port, Dublin stout and madeira to hand, but I don't fly so high, with me it's beer or white wine.' I said white wine, and he filled a glass for me, a glass of milk for himself, and dropped into the chair opposite me. He did so easily, gracefully, as though he were moving on the balls of his feet all the time. 'You're writing this article and you want to ask questions about Mr Wolfe, have I got it right?'

I produced the little tape recorder. He gave it a sideways glance.

'I'm not sure I trust those gadgets. Let's just bat it around a bit first about this piece.'

We talked for half an hour in the handsome apartment on the upper East Side, about my book on great detectives, who was going into it, whether they'd be compared with each other (he said, as he had done once before, that Nero Wolfe was 'the best detective north of the South Pole'). I stressed that my purpose was to give accounts of the lives and characters of my subjects, not to make comparisons. I sensed that I had passed some kind of test when he grinned, and said: 'There's no comparison. He was a genius, the rest were detectives. Would you like to see a photograph?'

I don't know exactly what I had expected, a monstrously fat man I suppose, since Wolfe at his heaviest weighed more than twenty stone. Anyway, I was surprised. The face was large and squarish, but not jowly or pudgy, the face of a big rather than a fat man. Brown hair and heavy-lidded brown eyes, a full mobile mouth, the expression amiable enough but a little threatening, not the face of a man who suffered fools at all, let alone suffering them gladly. It was the face of a heavyweight man, and if you liked heavyweights he could even have been called handsome. There were three photographs, all very similar, except that one showed him bending over an orchid, and revealed large shapely hands. None of the photographs was full length, so perhaps I didn't get the full impression of his bulk. I handed them back without comment.

'Now, Mr Symons, let's get down to cases. You've got questions you want to ask. Okay, I'll go along with you, but if there's anything I don't want to answer I'll say "No comment" like a politician, and you leave it at that. Or I'll ask you to stop the tape. If I say something I shouldn't and want it wiped, you wipe it there and then. Not that I don't trust you, just that being certain beats trusting people any day. Agreed?'

I agreed, and what follows is the text of our question-and-answer session. It suggests an explanation to the often-asked question 'What became of Nero Wolfe?', although the answer leaves an element of mystery.

JS I'd like you first to sketch verbally the lay-out at West 35th Street, what the place looked like and how it worked.

AG Okay, I'll try it. The house was an old brownstone, the number, well, it was somewhere between the 500s and the 900s. There were reasons for not giving the exact number then, and I guess they still apply. It was—

JS Excuse me. This book will be published in Britain and other countries besides the USA, and there are a lot of readers who don't know what a brownstone is. Even detectives. Like Hercule Poirot who asked "Enfin, what *is* a brownstone mansion? I have never known?"

AG I never thought those French detectives were much good. Okay, Belgian, I knew he was Belgian. If he was such a hot shot, why didn't he try his luck here in the States?

JS I couldn't tell you.

AG I could, but I won't. What's a brownstone? I never majored in architecture, but they're saying now that these brownstones are the city's pride and joy and so shouldn't be knocked down, the way almost everything in New York gets knocked down and replaced every twenty years or so. A brownstone is—well, most of them were put up around the turn of the century and they got the name because they were faced with sandstone. Mostly

they were built in whole rows like they were in West 35th Street, in three storeys plus a basement so that they had steps up from the sidewalk. I don't know that I can get nearer than that.

Our particular brownstone had seven steps up, and it was a double-width house —

JS In Britain we'd call it double fronted.

AG Would you now? Double-width makes a lot more sense. You went in the front door — if you could, that is, because it was always kept bolted except that time when Mr Wolfe got involved with Arnold Zeck. On your right was a coat rack, a real monster, eight feet wide, I don't know where it came from. Then the elevator which was tiny, four foot by six, but big enough to hold Mr Wolfe. Then the stairs, and past them the door to the dining room. This was a big room, made out of two, so it was forty feet long. That's the right side of the house. On the left as you went in there was first a door to a room looking on to the street, which didn't get much use. Then at the back the office, which is where we spent most of our time. You'd like me to say a bit more about the office?

JS Yes please. So much went on there, clients pulling guns or threatening to, getting knocked out, even dying there. Two of them in one case.

AG What was that? Oh yeah, I remember, *The Red Box*. Now, whatever I say about the office, you got to bear in mind that we lived in that house a good long time, and things were changed occasionally. And incidentally, don't ask me when Mr Wolfe bought the house (yes, he owned it) or when he set up as a consulting detective or when I started working for him, or any of that sort of stuff. I'm not going into all that, partly because my memory for dates was never good and is getting worse, partly because I think I've mixed up dates a bit sometimes, partly because it's the kind of stuff that bores me stiff. So, no dates. Happy?

JS Perfectly.

AG You don't look it. Where was I? Oh yeah, the office. It was a big rectangular room, living room as well as office. I liked it a lot, and so did Mr Wolfe. There was his desk, which was cherrywood, and his outsize chair which was upholstered in brown leather, and specially made for him by Meyer. I guess you know he had a kind of passion for yellow, and there was this bright yellow couch along one wall which had to be cleaned every couple of months. Yellow drapes of course. Then there was the red leather chair for clients, the one you've spotted. When we needed them, which was quite often because the office got crowded at times, I'd bring in chairs from the front room.

What else? Oh yeah, bookshelves by his desk of course, and a lot more on the opposite wall. Pictures of various sorts besides that listening panel. Maps, prints, pictures of Socrates and Shakespeare and a coal miner. Then there was my desk, with a typewriter that folded away. And in the far corner we had a place walled off to make a john and a washbowl for Wolfe. Saved him walking, as you know he didn't care too much for that. Did you notice I dropped the "Mr" then? Shows I'm getting used to you. You want more about the house? All right.

At the rear — we're still on the first floor, I believe it's your ground floor — there was the door to the kitchen where Fritz Brenner operated. The kitchen was big enough to eat in, and Wolfe spent a lot of time there. He made Fred Durkin eat out in the kitchen after he put vinegar into a specially prepared roux. Saul Panzer and Orrie Cather used to eat with us in the dining room. They were all operators he employed, you know that of course, though I've told you anyway. At the back there was a little yard, where Fritz grew tarragon, chives and stuff like that.

Downstairs was where Fritz slept, in a room that faced the street. You could get out that way, through a door under the front stoop. After a while Marko Vukcic, who was Wolfe's best friend, persuaded him to install a pool table down there, and every so often they'd play. The elevator went up to the plant rooms at the top. It stopped at the other floors, but young athletic types like me used the stairs. The plant rooms up top — well the roof up there was glassed in, and the orchidarium or

whatever you call it was partitioned into five rooms. Theo Horstmann looked after the ten thousand orchids that were Wolfe's pride and joy, and I kept the germination books which he was always pernickety about. Theo had to be very careful about the temperature and humidity of the orchids. He slept up there in a little den.

Upstairs, for a time we both had rooms on the second floor, me at the front, him at the back. Then I moved up a floor. What was his room like? Let me think. First impression you got was of that yellow he was nuts about. Yellow footboard to the bed, a streaky wood called anselmo that you don't see in England I guess. Yellow pyjamas — he always wore yellow socks too, remember that, and yellow shirts as well. Then, Heaven help us, a black silk coverlet. There he'd sit in the morning drinking chocolate or eating four pieces of toast with his eggs beurre noir (hope I'm pronouncing that right), and puffing his lips in and out. You needed a strong stomach to look at him in the morning. That's about it, I guess. There were a hundred other little details, like Wolfe having his own outsize chair in pretty well every room, the office, dining room, kitchen and plant room. Then there was a little red light outside his bedroom, an alarm connection which rang in my room. He and I had a running argument about whether I should have a noiseless typewriter. I won, because I was using it. And so on. If I told you all the different little things we'd be here the whole week. What next?

JS The average working day. What was it like?

AG It's all in the books. Ditto what I said before, we'd be here all week.

JS Even so, I'd like a few things which would help the illustrator. Did I tell you that the book's going to be illustrated? By an artist named Tom Adams? I'd be grateful if you could let me have a print of a couple of those photographs, and a couple of you. They'd help Tom a lot. Of course, he could come over here and paint you.

AG I couldn't sit still long enough. Besides, I don't want him painting an old dodderer. I'll let you have some prints, including one of me in my athletic prime.

JS Many thanks. Now, about the average day.

AG You have to understand there was no such thing. It's true there was a sort of routine. Wolfe had breakfast in bed at eight. Nine to eleven in the morning, four to six in the afternoon, he always spent in the plant rooms pretending to work, really admiring his own orchids. Lunch one to one thirty, dinner around seven fifteen, that was the idea. And another bit of the routine was his beer drinking. He drank too much beer. He'd start when he came down from the plant rooms, and with a break or two go on steadily until bedtime. When he'd had seven after dinner, I'd sometimes suggest that was enough, but he didn't take kindly to being told things. He'd just look at me out of those heavy-lidded eyes and press the button on his desk for Fritz to bring in another. Hell, I forgot about the button. That's the kind of thing I mean, you're bound to forget something. Also routine was his reading. He often read two or three books at once, around thirty pages of each at a time. I'm no reader, but I guess you wouldn't find many bookworms behaving like outsize butterflies.

So that was Wolfe's routine. How about mine? A lot of the time I was at the typewriter dealing with correspondence. There's not much about that in the books, because what's there to say? I might be working on the germination records, which forever needed keeping up to date. Then if we had a case on, and mostly there was some sort of case on hand, I'd be acting as a legman, maybe talking to Lon Cohen who was on the city desk at the *Gazette*, chatting with witnesses, checking on the movements of suspects, and so on. Wolfe was the brain, I was the arms and legs, I never pretended anything else or wanted it any other way. I think I said somewhere I collected pieces of the puzzle for Wolfe to work on. Times I had nothing to do, I'd go out to the kitchen, talk to Fritz, watch him preparing food. Fritz was a genius in his way, which meant there were two of 'em in the house.

Now you might say that was our average life, but as I said at the start you'd be wrong. You'll see from the books that routine was always being interrupted, Inspector Cramer coming around to complain or get information or just to talk, clients who had to see Wolfe in the next ten minutes, threats, attempted shootings, all sorts. We had the orchid rooms machine-gunned once, we had a man who'd asked to stay the night blown up by a bomb. Even a statement like Wolfe's saying "I never leave my home on business" wasn't literally true. If you read the books you'll see he left it, at a rough guess, a dozen times or more. So there was no average day. Just add up all it says in the books, that was our lives.

JS Not altogether. You've left out food.

AG (Laughing) Oh yes. That's in the books too. And how. But don't expect Archie Goodwin to talk about the food. He was lucky enough to eat it.

JS There are a couple of points I'd like to ask about. I began to make a note of all the dishes mentioned, though I didn't carry it through. But I was struck by Wolfe's attachment to sausage in various forms. You'll remember his anxiety to get some from "the best sausage maker west of Cherbourg", the sausage with ten kinds of herbs in it, the fuss he made about analysing *saucisse minuit*, and his triumph when he finally got the recipe. And that's only the beginnings of the tale of sausage. Now I like sausages myself, although I've hardly ever found an American sausage worth eating, but no high-class chef would put a sausage dish anywhere near the top among his recipes.

AG No comment. Except that you've never eaten sausages prepared by Fritz.

JS I wish I had. But going through the meals, as I say, I noticed a certain monotony and heaviness about them. One lunch, for example, consisted of corn cakes with breaded pork tenderloin, followed by corn cakes with hot tomato and cheese sauce, and then corn cakes with honey. Too many corn cakes, I'd say. And although Wolfe's taste was modified later on, it always tended to the robust and spicy rather than the delicate. Squirrel stew with black sauce, fried shrimps and Cape Cod clam cakes with a sour sauce thickened by mushrooms, kid goulash, they're typical dishes. I suppose you might say they're a blend of Wolfe's Montenegrin origins and his acquired American tastes, but when it comes to him eating a whole ten-pound goose between eight o'clock and midnight, you've got to call Wolfe a gourmand rather than a gourmet.

AG You're doing the calling. I must be mistaken. I thought the idea was you were interviewing me.

JS You don't have any view about this? I get the impression sometimes that your own tastes were simpler. When Wolfe was having his breakfast eggs prepared in some complicated fashion, you were happy with eggs sunny side up, broiled ham, and pancakes, a traditional American breakfast.

AG No comment, except that you weren't there and you don't know. Oh yeah, one other thing. I've never been in England, but they tell me the national dishes are beef so tough saws break their teeth on it, and overcooked cabbage. Fritz had fifteen ways with cabbage, but he was too kind-hearted ever to boil it to death.

JS Tell me a little about Fritz, and some of the others.

AG I repeat, Fritz Brenner was a genius. Wolfe paid him $1000 a month, which was more than he paid me, but Fritz was worth it. He was a little Swiss, acted as cook, housekeeper and grocer, and unlike you shared Wolfe's passion for sausage. He used to blush when his food was praised. Wore butler shoes, came from the part of Switzerland where they speak French, and read French newspapers even though he'd lived all those years in the States. I can't say too much for him.

Then there were the free-lance operatives. Saul Panzer was the best by a long shot. Little man with a big nose, had a horrible-smelling light brown cigar sticking out of his tiny wrinkled mug as often as not, but certainly he was good. Never let go when he had his teeth into a job. He was worth what Wolfe paid him, which went up from $30 a day to $70 or $80. The others I didn't go for so much. Orrie Cather was slim and handsome when we first used him, lost some hair later. I can't say I ever liked him.

JS And how right you were.
AG You could say that. Fred Durkin was Irish, and I've mentioned his eating habits. Bill Gore and Johnny Keems were all right as long as you spelled out what you wanted in words of one syllable. Then there were the cops. Lieutenant Rowcliffe always thought my permanent home should have been a prison cell, and I loved him too. Purley Stebbins was the kind you feel, well, you can take him or leave him, and on the whole I preferred to leave him. Most of the the top brass were energetic, and that's the best you could say for them. Wolfe popped one of them named Ash on the jaw, when Ash laid a hand on him. That leaves our Fergus, Fergus Cramer, onetime head of the Homicide Bureau. It could be there was a lot to be said for Fergus, though I didn't often get around to saying it. He was chunky, about my height, wrinkled pink skin which could look bright red when he lost his temper, sharp grey-blue eyes. He wasn't too bright, but he shone like an arc-lamp compared to the rest of them. He was honest. And he respected Wolfe, I'd even say he knew Wolfe was a genius. That was Fergus's saving grace. How am I doing?
JS Wonderful. It all helps to fill the picture, even when you may feel I should know it anyway. There's another thing. You went around with all sorts and sizes of women, and obviously they all found you attractive from Lily Rowan downwards if that's the right word, but there's no mention of one ever staying the night in your room. Or of you renting a room to carry on an affair. You make it clear in twenty different books that Wolfe didn't like women. He said once, "They are astounding and successful animals," and that's a typical comment. I'd say he was afraid of them at heart. But what I'd like to know is whether at West 35th Street he absolutely forbade you to have women staying the night. And if so, what did you feel about it?
AG Turn that damned thing off.

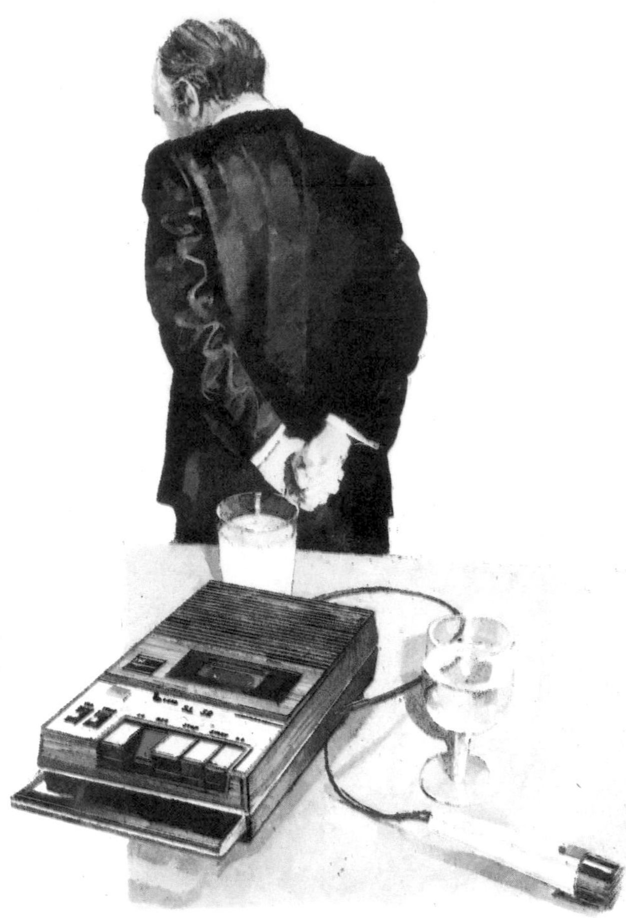

I did so. Archie Goodwin got up, walked up and down the room a couple of times with his fists clenched. He did not look at me, and I felt a little nervous. Then he asked if I would like another glass of wine, and I said yes. When he'd brought it, and more milk for himself, he sat down again and looked at me, frowning. When he spoke, though, the words were mild.

'I hoped you wouldn't put that kind of question. I asked around about you when I had your letter saying you'd like to see me, because frankly your name didn't mean a thing to me.' He gave his engaging grin.

'I'll tell you what I learned. You're a hot-shot British crime writer, and they say a kind of crime historian too. Got a lot of prejudices, though, and sometimes you make allegations that give offence. Here's something I'd like you to explain.' He took a piece of paper from his pocket, and read: '"There seemed something sexually ambiguous about the household of Nero Wolfe and Archie Goodwin." You wrote that. I nodded. 'What the hell's it supposed to mean? That Wolfe and I were that way, that I was his boy, is that what it means?'

I swallowed. 'It means what it says. Almost everybody of your age, most people of Wolfe's age, have a sex life. According to you Wolfe never had one, or if he had you don't mention it. If you had one, it wasn't connected with the old brownstone. It was a sexually ambiguous household, and I wondered what you did about sex, that's all.'

For a few moments I was unsure of his reaction. Then I got the Goodwin grin.

'If Wolfe were here — and it would be Mr Wolfe to you — he'd say you were impertinent, and he'd be right. His relationship with me was father and son, if you can understand anything that simple. He was twenty-four years older than me, so he could have been my father, although in fact my old man's name was Titus and he was a farmer in Ohio. Wolfe looked after me the way a father should look after his son, and anything I am I owe to him. He could make me mad, but I've said often enough that my heart gave an extra thump when he said "Satisfactory, Archie." As for anything that happened between me and Lily, or any other girls, that's between the girls and me and the four-poster. So far as Wolfe's concerned you might add the word celibacy to your vocabulary. And if you say that doesn't answer your question, it's the only answer you're going to get.'

'Would you mind if I included this bit of conversation in my book?'

At that he laughed outright. 'I'll be damned if you haven't got a nerve. All right. Subject now closed.'

'One more question. Did you marry Lily Rowan?'

He shook his head. 'Her nor anybody else. A long time ago I said I'd seen dozens of girls I wouldn't mind marrying, and whenever I meet a new one I'm interested and alive to all the possibilities, but I never seem to get infatuated. That still goes. Subject completely closed.'

With that we went back to the tape.

JS That covers the background. People who want every single detail, how many times you were arrested, how many people died in the office (something like a dozen by my reckoning) can read the books and stories. I want to move on to Wolfe's personality. And his weight. He seems never to have taken any exercise, you only have to look at Fritz's menus to see he ate fattening foods, yet he appears to have stayed fit. Are you sure you didn't exaggerate his weight?

AG No exaggeration, that's the way it was. And yes, it may have been all against the odds, but he did stay fit. You might say natural laws were suspended for Nero Wolfe.

JS All right. Now, background and personality. I know you don't want to fuss with dates, but he was born in Montenegro, place unknown, went to school there, knew Marko Vukcic from boyhood. He was in the Austrian intelligence service during World War I, set up as a detective some time in the late twenties, maybe 1928. Is all that agreed?

AG It certainly isn't. It can't be agreed, as you call it, by me, because I wasn't there and don't know. I can certify that he had young relatives in Belgrade, because I used to type letters to them. But you've read the works and know the things people have said. One theory is that Marko wasn't Wolfe's friend but his twin brother, and that they were born in Trenton, New Jersey, and went out to Montenegro when they were very small. There's also a view that Wolfe was the illegitimate son of Sherlock Holmes and Irene Adler. If you ask me, most of those ideas range from way out to plain crazy, but I don't *know*. No more does anybody else.

JS Wolfe said once that he'd been in a dirty jail in Algiers. You can't verify that?

AG No. I don't know whether he had a house in Egypt either. He *said* he had, and once threatened to go and live there, but that could have been said just for effect. He'd say all kinds of things and pull all sorts of tricks in the course of a case. You must have noticed that.

JS I have. What about his personality? He said himself "I am congenitally tart and thorny," and often talked about his own genius. You give lots of instances when he was rude, boorish, dictatorial, and in almost every story you use a phrase like "cocky and unlimited conceit" in talking about him. This all seems to add up to something disagreeable, yet most of the people who knew him well seem to have loved him.

AG Cramer and other assorted policemen excepted. I can't explain that, can't begin to explain it.

JS It seems a contradiction.

AG Somebody or other said "Do I contradict myself? Very well then, I contradict myself." I can only tell it the way it was. Sure, he ate too much, could be rude and even brutal, he was lazy—I remember saying once that his idea of paradise was being able to take no jobs for months, sit around reading books and propagating orchids—but still Fritz, and I guess Saul Panzer and maybe half-a-dozen others would happily have given their lives for him. Not to mention me.

JS I seem to have run out of questions. Thank you very much, Mr Goodwin. There are lots of other things I could ask, like why you said at one time that there were two people who called him Nero, and at another time that there were three, but I think questions like that would just be confusing. Of course, you know there's one matter I'd like to talk about that's never been made public. Is Nero Wolfe dead? I suppose so.

AG I couldn't say that.

JS Then he's alive?

AG I don't know that either. I can't see it would do any harm to tell the story now. That's if you want to hear it.

JS You must be joking.

AG All right. It began with a 'phone call. I'm not going to give you names, I'll only say that it wasn't the President's office, but if you take one step down from there, then you've got it. A voice stuffed with cottonwool said that his master—he actually said that, just like a Britisher—would be grateful if Mr Wolfe could spare an hour of his time. I was all set to go into my usual spiel when cottonwool said that they knew Mr Wolfe never left his home on business, and that his master would like to make an appointment to come to the office, and the matter was urgent. Things were slack, and I fixed it for that same day at six, when Wolfe came down from the plant rooms.

A couple of minutes before six the visitor arrived. We've had some big fish calling on us—you'll remember the one who arrived at the end of *The Doorbell Rang*—but none bigger than this one. He was alone, and as he gave me his coat he said "You're Archie Goodwin," and shook hands. As we went into the office we heard the whirr of the elevator. When Wolfe came in the VIP just smiled. He'd obviously been told that shaking hands wasn't the right approach. Wolfe pressed the desk button for Fritz to bring beer, offered our visitor a selection of drinks which he refused, and when the beer was in the glass said "Now, sir, I understand you wish to consult me."

The VIP leaned forward. "Mr Wolfe, this is a matter of international importance. I know that Mr Goodwin is your trusted assistant, but in this case I should appreciate it if we might speak alone, at least at first."

"My dear sir, you have evidently taken the trouble to acquaint yourself with my habits and way of life. You must know that I am hamstrung without Mr Goodwin, and that if I were to accede to your request I should give him the details of your interview immediately you left."

"Very well. I reluctantly agree that Mr Goodwin shall stay. But I must impress on you both that nothing said in this room must be mentioned outside it."

Wolfe was impatient. "Pfui. You have already decided that we are trustworthy, or you would not be here. Very well then, trust us."

The VIP smiled. "Someone in my position gets used to evasion and circumlocution. I'll ask you to be patient while I go over a little of your own political background. I assure you I have reasons for doing so. You favour federalism as a principle, you have for a long time supported a group in favour of World Government. You once called yourself an anarchist, and although Mr Goodwin thought you were being whimsical, I believe an element of seriousness was there too. You dislike most forms of authority, including the FBI. Correct so far?" Wolfe inclined his head.

"In World War II you and Mr Goodwin both served your country, Mr Goodwin as a Major in US Military Intelligence, you as a civilian in G2. Mr Goodwin made three applications to go overseas, all of them turned down because of his usefulness here. You, Mr Wolfe, have eight languages including Serbo-Croat. You spent your youth in Yugoslavia, and know the country well." I was beginning to think he liked the sound of his own voice too much, when he wound up. "Some years ago you paid a visit to Yugoslavia."

"Your statements are correct." Wolfe had finished his beer, and was becoming impatient. "Your purpose in recounting them remains obscure."

The VIP took a breath, came out with it in a rush. "We want you to go there again on behalf of the Government, and make contact with a resistance group. There is a good chance of overthrowing the present régime, and replacing it by a genuinely democratic Government."

I can't remember any other occasion on which I had seen Wolfe at a loss for words. He rang the bell again, got two more beers and poured one. I waited for him to explode. Instead he said, quietly enough: "You know what happened before?"

The VIP coughed. "You went to find the murderer of your best friend, Marko Vukcic. And you succeeded."

Wolfe considered, with his lips pushing in and out in the way that showed he was thinking hard. In the end he said, "Marko also hoped to overthrow the régime. His enterprise was hopeless, and I said so. I told my adopted daughter Carla the same thing, but she refused to listen. My visit was a private matter, but theirs was a public enterprise and it failed. Why should things be different this time?"

The VIP leaned forward, a gleam in his eye like the look in a fisherman's when he sees the bait has been taken. "Because this time there has been proper preparation. And your friend Marko was an amateur. This time the planning has been in the hands of professionals."

There were times when Wolfe would have blasted anybody who made a remark like that, but this wasn't one of them. He stayed silent, and I believe I understood his thoughts, or some of them. He had always refused to become involved in Marko's project, and when his friend was shot down in New York and Wolfe went to the morgue and put two old dinars over Marko's eyes, I believe he felt remorse. Mind you, that was guessing, because he'd never talked about it. Now his eyelids lowered so that he might have been asleep, but his lips formed words. I couldn't swear to them, although they might have been: "Marko ... the past." Then his head moved up slowly, as though on a spring.

"I am conspicuous. You have thought of that?"

"A positive advantage. We want to make our presence known. You would be that presence." Our visitor smiled, then added: "There would be an element of personal danger." Wolfe nodded. "You would be rendering a service to this country, but a much greater one to the country of your origin. If this uprising succeeds — "

"There is no need to play the patriotic tune, or to labour the obvious," Wolfe growled. "Very well. I accept. You will inform me of what you expect from me. I shall require a week for preparation. And I should like Mr Goodwin to accompany me, although I must not take his acceptance for granted. Archie?"

I gulped. "I can hardly wait."

I'll cut out most of the to-and-froing of the next week, or we shall be here all night. Part of it Wolfe spent being briefed about what was expected. As far as I understood it the idea was that the presence of an American, known to have official backing would bring the waverers, if any, over to the side of the Heroes of Montenegro, which was the name of the resistance group. (The one before had been called something just as fancy, the Spirit of the Black Mountain.) Its leader's name was Popovic. Wolfe would be in touch with an important Government official named Vizin, which as their names go is an easy one to pronounce. Vizin was Number Five or Six in the régime, and wanted to become Number One. If you think that's a cynical view, well, it's the view I took. The way Vizin had sold it to our VIP, the country was ripe for a change of Government as soon as he dropped his hat.

All this condenses hours of briefings, and about a hundred memos marked "Top Secret", "Eat When Read", and so on. I must say Wolfe survived them well.

In fact, it wouldn't be too much to say he amazed me. Of course we'd done most of the routine before, on the previous trip, but I never thought he'd do it again. He left the house on his own without complaint, cut out carbohydrates and root vegetables, and told Fritz that where possible all main dishes were to be served plain broiled, with no sauces. In the week before we left he took off twenty pounds. Mind you, there was still a lot left.

A couple of cases we had on hand were given up, and he did one thing he hadn't done before. He drew up a will. I won't go into all the details, but the brownstone was left to me outright, with any of the things in it that I wanted. Fritz got enough to start his own restaurant, or retire if he felt like it. Everyone was remembered, from Theo, Saul Panzer and Fred Durkin, to Charley the cleaning man. Cramer, who was suffering badly from arthritis, was left his Montenegrin applewood cane. Wolfe had Fritz and Theo in tears when he told them of the bequests. I stayed dry-eyed, because I knew he'd like it that way. When he said he was glad I had avoided any embarrassing display of sentiment, I told him I couldn't understand why he was making such a to-do.

"In what you called your mortal encounter with Arnold Zeck you disappeared, took off over a hundred pounds and acquired a new personality, but I don't recollect you making a will. And you didn't make one when we went out to this

benighted country before, so what's all this stuff about wills? Just look at me, I'm not making a will, not even taking a tearful leave of Lily Rowan."

These reasonable remarks got only grunts for reply. One clause in the will said that its provisions were to come into operation if nothing was heard of him for three years. I remembered that afterwards.

When the week was up we left for Europe by plane. The previous time we'd flown New York-London-Rome, and then crossed from Bari. Now we got a flight direct to Belgrade. In the plane Wolfe was tight-lipped, didn't talk, wouldn't touch the food that tastes of plastic even though it may look like lox or prime ribs. Part of the time he read Rebecca West's *Black Lamb and Grey Falcon*, the rest of it he pretended to sleep. Maybe he did sleep. I know I didn't. As we were coming down he opened his eyes. He would have held on to the sides of his chair, except that one arm rest had been lowered so that he could have two seats. Even with his reduced weight he couldn't fit into one.

"Are we there?"

"Just touching down." We did, not that smoothly, I'll allow. He made a sound like a mortally wounded balloon.

"Archie, I shall never enter one of these machines again."

So how are we going to get home, I felt inclined to ask. But didn't.

In Belgrade Wolfe had an address given him by the VIP, and there we made contact with a small dark fellow whose name was something like Morstan. I gathered he was the movement's big wheel in the capital, except for Vizin of course. Wolfe said he was intelligent, but since they talked in Serbo-Croat I couldn't confirm that. In fact, things were just the way they had been on our other visit. Maybe I should have brushed up on my Serbo-Croat or my Slovene during the intervening years, but not foreseeing the necessity I hadn't. The result was that I couldn't understand a thing anybody said, which I didn't care for at all. You might say I was downright miserable. On the other hand Wolfe's spirits improved from the moment we landed. He gave up his semi-starvation diet, and was enthusiastic about several dishes, like the mixed meat done into sausage shapes, and bits of meat roasted on a skewer, things that would have shocked Fritz by their crudity.

Wolfe graciously allowed me to drive the car that was provided for us. I forget who the man was who said that any car driver in Yugoslavia had one foot in prison and the other in the grave, but certainly a lot of the roads are bad, almost all the driving is wild, and if you're involved in an accident they tend to slap you in a cell first and discuss who's to blame afterwards.

However, we avoided hitting anything. We

drove from Belgrade through a lot of woods, then into mountains. It wasn't so many miles from Mount Lovchen, where we'd been before. We went on a quite decent road through villages whose names I won't attempt to pronounce, along something called the Lim valley. There was a lot of beautiful country, and some odd things like shepherds with movable huts that go along on runners. We finished that day at a hotel in a little place called Ivangrad. The hotel was clean, but you couldn't say much more for it. The hot water ran cold, and you had to walk the hell of a long corridor to reach the toilet. The food was the usual meat on a skewer. None of it fazed Wolfe. He was in tremendous spirits.

"Do you know how I can be sure we are back in Montenegro, Archie? Because the men are taller and more handsome. They say two things about Montenegrin men. One is that they are the tallest and most handsome in the world, the other that they are the laziest." I grunted. With Wolfe this loquacious, I reckoned it was my turn. "Did you see that waiter at dinner? You don't find his kind of dignity except where there is a tradition of independence. Marko and I spent some of our youth in the place where we are going to-morrow."

"Very interesting. Where would that be, and why are we going there?"

"It is up in the mountains. There I meet Vizin. He will take me to a meeting with Popovic."

"Just Popovic, nobody else?"

"He is the important man here. The rest – pfui." He waved a dismissive hand. "We shall co-ordinate the time of the uprising. It begins in Montenegro, and then it will spread like a forest fire."

"If it's going to spread that fast, what are we doing here?"

"We're here to convince them that we are ready to help with arms and supplies just as soon as they give the signal."

I didn't like it, the whole thing smelled bad to me, but what could I do except drive the car? And believe me, it wasn't a joy ride. From Ivangrad we went along some of the craziest roads I've ever seen, double hairpins with no room to pass and a sheer drop the other side down three thousand feet of mountain. If we'd met another car, one of us would have had to back around a road that was problem enough going forward, but luckily there were only a few sheep that scrambled up the rocks. At last we reached a small plateau. Wolfe told me to stop, and we both got out. Mountains rose above us, we were on the plateau, and then on the other side there was a drop to a deep valley and then more mountains. It was very still, and the stillness got to you. Majestic isn't a word I often use, but I guess you could say it was majestic. And Wolfe was majestic too, as he stood there taking it all in. There was a look on his face I'd never seen, wistfulness, longing, I don't know what you'd call it.

"Where are we?" I asked, for something to say.

"At the beginning of the Cakor Pass. The roof of Yugoslavia. I've been here with Marko, hunting dragonflies. I know it well."

The road we'd been on ended at the plateau. At the other side there was a steep track among the rocks, no more than four or five feet wide. Up this track came a man riding one mule and leading another. He was a big square-headed fellow wearing a cap. Wolfe greeted him, and they talked a bit. Then Wolfe turned to me.

"I presume this is Vizin," I said. "But don't tell me you're going on the back of that mule."

"Of course I am. What else do you suggest?"

"It's cruelty to mules. He'll sink under the weight. Or go on strike. I hear mules are great at refusing to move."

He looked at me, said "Goodbye, Archie." Then — and this was Nero Wolfe who hated even a touch on his arm and wouldn't shake hands — he clasped me in his arms European style, and I felt the warmth of his face against mine. Then he was on the back of the mule, and they were going down the rocky track. I watched them till they were out of sight. I never saw him again.

In which Archie Goodwin Remembers

Archie gestured for me to turn off the tape recorder. I said, 'But what happened?'

'I don't know. Wolfe said that he'd get news to me at Ivangrad, so I went back there, waited the best part of a week. The hell of it was, not knowing the language I couldn't find out a thing. Then I drove back to Belgrade and got hold of an English-language newspaper, but couldn't find a thing in it about Yugoslavia. Finally I reached some third secretary in the American Embassy. I couldn't say much about Wolfe because the mission was confidential, but there'd been no uprising. After a lot of pestering I found out that there was a story tucked away inside one of the official papers about the leader of a Montenegrin separatist movement being ambushed and shot, it was thought by some rival terrorists, as they were called. I waited around in Belgrade for a while, then flew home. Tried to see the VIP who'd visited us, but never made it. My cottonwool chum said they had no information about Mr Wolfe.

'And that was all, except that for months I went on beating my head against official blank walls. We waited the three years and heard nothing, so the terms of the will operated. We all wished they hadn't.'

'So it was all a plot by the Yugoslav Government to kill Popovic. You said he was the only important man.'

'Perhaps. But why would the American Government or even one of its agencies join a plot like that?'

'Or Vizin tricked your VIP into sending Wolfe, used him as a bait to trap Popovic, and had them both killed.'

'Maybe.'

I hesitated. 'Or Wolfe got away. He was never deceived — nobody ever fooled Nero Wolfe. He guessed there was something wrong about the scheme from the start, but he'd made up his mind that he wanted to be back in his homeland. He decided in advance that he wouldn't come back. That's why he made the will.'

'I like that one best. I don't know the truth, and I guess I never shall, but I like to think he's out there, hunting dragonflies up on the roof of Yugoslavia.'

ELLERY
RICHARD

Which Expounds the Ellery Queens Mystery

In the seven biographical sketches of this volume no figure has appeared so baffling as Ellery Queen. It is not that information about him is lacking, although there are some surprising gaps in the family history, but rather that what we learn is sometimes so contradictory that the biographer has to abandon exposition for interpretation—interpretation which leads to an astonishing conclusion. First of all, however, let me outline some of the facts given us in the thirty-some novels and short story collections that have Ellery Queen's name on the cover.

I put it in that way because Ellery Queen was not in fact the author of the early tales that bear his name. They are, rather, told by him to a gentleman who is identified no further than as 'JJ McC', and then put by JJ McC into fictional form with the help of records in the New York Police Department. The prefatory notes written by JJ McC are often of great interest. In the first Queen story given to the public, *The Roman Hat Mystery*, JJ McC tells of finding himself in an Italian mountain village, and there meeting by chance his old friends the Queens: specifically, the former Inspector Richard Queen, his son Ellery, the 'glorious creature' to whom Ellery was married, their infant son who 'resembled his grandfather to an extraordinary degree', and their orphan boy-of-all-work Djuna.

The Queens have retired from the detection of crime, and give the impression of being firmly settled in Italy. Their home on West 87th Street is now 'a semi-private museum of curios collected during their productive years'. We are told of the fine portrait of father and son by Thiraud, the Inspector's precious antique Florentine snuff-box, and other things. JJ McC's comments in later books confirm the retirement and give further details. We are told that Queen is not the real family name, and that father and son were 'integral, I might even say major, cogs in the wheel of New York City's police machinery', particularly during the second and third decades of this century. *The second and third decades*—that means between 1910 and 1930. We realize immediately, since no story is set before the late twenties, and several take place during or after World War II, that contradictions exist. I may as well say here that I cannot explain this one, except by the supposition that J J McC was deliberately deceiving us, for it is clear from the characters' speech and behaviour that the publication dates of the early Queen mysteries are correct, and that the *Roman Hat*, *French Powder*, *Dutch Shoe* and other mysteries took place in the late twenties and early thirties.

Happily, we have a detailed description of the New York home before it became a museum. Father and son lived on the top floor of a late Victorian brownstone on West 87th Street. Behind a big oak door marked 'The Queens' was a small, narrow foyer, with a tapestry depicting the chase which covered the whole of one wall. Beneath the tapestry was a heavy mission table, a parchment lamp, and on the table a pair of bronze book-ends holding a three-volume set of the *Arabian Nights Entertainments*. Two mission chairs and a small rug completed the foyer, the sombreness of which contrasted wonderfully with the cheerful large living room. This was lined on three sides by bookcases which rose tier upon tier to the high ceiling. On the fourth wall was a large natural fireplace, with an iron grate and a solid oak beam for mantel. Over the fireplace crossed sabres, given to the Inspector by his old fencing master of Nuremberg, provided a reminiscence of student days. Lamps, easy chairs, an old walnut table and bright cushions completed the room in which most of the Queens' time was spent. A swing door led out from it to the kitchen. Ellery and his father each had a bedroom, and there was a small room for Djuna.

The Queens' apartment could hardly compare with Nero Wolfe's house fifty-two blocks south as the scene of mayhem. Perhaps the most violent thing that happened there was the invasion of the apartment by two men who carried the Queens off to their assignment with the remarkable Bendigos. We have very clear portraits of the two principal inhabitants. Inspector Richard Queen is no more than five feet four inches tall (as with Poirot, he must have evaded the police height regulations), stoops a little, takes snuff frequently, has thick grey hair and moustache, grey eyes and delicate hands. He looks mild, but is very alert, brisk and competent. His attention to detail is unwavering, his patience almost endless. About Richard Queen's parentage we know nothing, and of his early life before entering the police no more than that he was a student in Germany. He recognizes his son's superior intellectual capacity, and his attitude to it is almost one of reverence. The very last words in one of the early books, spoken by the Inspector, are: 'Ellery's brains . . . my stupidity . . . '

The Inspector's over-modest denigration of his own talents receives Ellery's occasionally supercilious consent. (It should be emphasized that we are still talking of the early cases.) It cannot be said that Ellery is disrespectful to the father he often calls Pater, but he shows too obvious an awareness of his own genius. 'Poor dad!' he says pityingly on one occasion. 'He's an excellent policeman, but he has no vision, no imagination. You need imagination in this business.' In the course of another case he calls his father 'good Polonius'. Ellery went to Harvard, and we must, I am afraid, call him at this time a Harvard snob.

There is no doubt, however, about the extent of his learning. This is perhaps most evident in *The Greek Coffin Mystery* which, although the fourth Queen adventure to be published, occurred only just after Ellery had graduated. Here he quotes Goethe in German and Rousseau in French, and he shows familiarity here and in other early cases with Homer, Plato, Ovid, Colley Cibber, Napoleon, Euripides, Byron . . . the list is long. He is likely to begin a comment on some aspect of the mystery by saying 'I'm with Kant at least to this extent,' or 'Old Publius Syrus knew what he was talking about,' and his forms of speech are often polysyllabically jocose, as when he calls a secretary 'the charming amanuensis of our defunct mysterioso'. Yet although Ellery might be called an affected young man, there is no doubt of his genius in making logical deductions from the given evidence, and reaching conclusions which are only apparent after he has made them. I should count myself among those who feel that his genius was never more finely displayed than in the *Dutch Shoe*, *Greek Coffin* and *Egyptian Cross* mysteries.

In person Ellery is six inches taller than his father, slender and elegant, with 'a hint of Bond Street' about his clothes. His silver-grey eyes are alert behind rimless pince-nez, which he wears on a chain. He frequently twirls these pince-nez, or polishes them with a gentle circular motion, while he is considering a particularly bothersome point. He carries a light stick, and smokes both a pipe and cigarettes, becoming a chain smoker at difficult times. He does not drive a car in New York, but once outside city limits may be seen at the wheel of a Duesenberg. This is a two-seater open model, *circa* 1924, with a rumble seat at the back. When driving the Duesenberg in winter, even with the top and side curtains up, Ellery sometimes wears an old raccoon coat with fur earflaps.

Ellery likes a drink, but there is no suggestion that he has ever taken a glass too much. He has an eye for the ladies, and they for him. He calls Irene Sewell in *The Chinese Orange Mystery* a fascinating wench, and is said by Rosa Godfrey in *The Spanish Cape Mystery* to be almost handsome when he removes his pince-nez. All of these cases must have preceded his marriage, because he met his wife during the case of the Mimic Murders (which has never been given to the public), and took her off to Italy. He is also in his spare time a writer of detective stories, among which are to be counted *The Affair of the Black Window* and *Murder of the*

Marionettes. I have never found either of these books.

The New York establishment is completed by Djuna, of whose background we know little more than that he has been an orphan for as long as he can remember, and that he loves the Inspector and reveres Ellery. Ellery has been known to call him Djuna the Magnificent, and we are told that he is a cook with a flair for new gastronomic creations.

* * *

It is usual for critics to divide the Queen adventures into groups, and to say that the first Queen period ended with the tenth book, *Halfway House*. Francis M Nevins, in his comprehensive study *Royal Bloodline*, indeed discovers four distinct periods in the stories. What Mr Nevins has missed, however, along with other critics, is the fact that in almost all of the stories after *Halfway House* Ellery Queen is manifestly a *different person*. The reason for my title may now be apparent. Just as it seems more likely that there were two Oswalds with each new discovery made about the Kennedy assassination, so there were two Ellery Queens.

I have already said that there are contradictions in the Queen canon, and it is time to enumerate them. The first Ellery Queen wore pince-nez and carried a stick, the second Ellery (found for example in *Cat of Many Tails*, *Double Double*, *The Origin of Evil*) has neither. Such appendages are important. We are told, for example, that *The Finishing Stroke* was Ellery's first case, but the fact that in it Ellery uses neither stick nor pince-nez is one of the factors that make this undoubtedly the first case of Ellery II. There are many differences, once we look for them. Ellery I uses forms of speech that are individual and sometimes affected, Ellery II talks like most educated Americans. Ellery I drinks only modestly, Ellery II shares a bottle of brandy with the latest Hollywood genius Jacques Butcher, and emerges well and truly sloshed. Ellery II abjures those quotations so much loved by Ellery I. Ellery I is never seen to fail in his deductions, while Ellery II more than once reproaches himself for his failures. 'Here I sit, over the grave of my second victim,' he reflects at the end of one case. The attitudes of Ellery I and Ellery II to crime are different. Near the end of *The Spanish Cape Mystery* Ellery I says that: 'I choose to close my mind to the human elements, and treat it as a problem in mathematics. The fate of the murderer I leave to those who decide such things.' In *The Door Between* Ellery II, after having induced a killer to commit suicide by himself perpetrating an act of forgery, reflects uneasily on what he has done, and thinks that 'It was too much like playing God to feel entirely comfortable.'

Ellery II lacks something of his predecessor's detective skills. He fails to solve the puzzle of *The Finishing Stroke* for more than a quarter of a century. At times he has to be guided by the Inspector to a conclusion, and in *The Fourth Side of the Triangle* he is positively 'saved from intellectual error by his long-suffering father', as Mr Nevins puts it. Ellery II shows none of Ellery I's arrogance in talking to or about the Inspector, and of course no longer calls him Pater. They deal with each other as equals.

Those are some of the many contradictions. Others become apparent as soon as one looks closely into the cases, like the fact that Ellery I writes detective stories, while Ellery II is always working on 'a novel'. How can they be explained? My interpretation is that there were, not metaphorically but in the most literal sense, two detectival Ellery Queens. I have called the second Ellery II, but he may better be given the traditional symbol of the unknown, X. Ellery was concerned with the ten cases that ended with *Halfway House*, and with most of the affairs recounted in short stories, X Queen with the rest. Ellery retired to married life in Italy, and thereafter the central character is X. I looked for errors in my interpretation, and it is fair to say that I found a few — a very few — passages that seemed to contradict it. In *Calamity Town*, which like all the New England

Wrightsville stories is an investigation carried out by X Queen, the pince-nez are mentioned, although the stick is not. Such minor exceptions are to be explained by the difficulty that J J McC must have experienced (it is my view that he continued to record the adventures, even though no longer writing prefaces to them) in making the transition. It is remarkable that the whole thing has been carried through so smoothly that no previous commentator has noticed the existence of a second personality carrying on the famous Ellery Queen name.

If further proof were needed, it would lie in the two men's different attitudes to women. 'I've known some that were passable,' Ellery says condescendingly. Compare this with X's feelings at sight of Paula Paris, the Hollywood gossip writer of a column called 'Seeing Stars'. Paula Paris was, X says, the most beautiful woman he had ever met:

> He had always considered himself immune to the grand passion; even the most attractive of her sex had never meant more to him than someone to open doors for or help in and out of taxis. But at this historic moment misogyny, that crusted armor, inexplicably cracked and fell away from him, leaving him defenceless.

It is obvious that this can hardly be the man who has a wife and child waiting for him in Italy. X is besotted with Paula, and cures her of the 'crowd phobia' which makes her refuse to go out. She accompanies him to race tracks, baseball and football games, and on such sporting occasions X reveals a passion for sport quite alien to Ellery. 'Never missed a New York series before,' he complains to Paula out in Hollywood, where he is working for a film studio. When she books a flight for them to see the game he 'wires Dad to snare a box', and at the game eats peanuts and frankfurters, and says reverently that Big Bill Tree (who is shortly to be murdered) was 'the greatest left-handed pitcher major league baseball ever saw'. But although cured of misogyny, X stops short of marriage. When Paula asks, in response to a piece of gallantry, whether he will say such pretty things when they are married, he turns pale and chokes, until she says that she didn't mean it. Whatever may be X's relationship with Paula, he is far more susceptible to women than Ellery ever was: witness his feelings about Pat Wright in *Calamity Town* ('that hair of yours drives me quite mad') and Delia Priam in *The Origin of Evil* ('I'm not a skunk, Delia, and you're not a tramp').

The textual evidence is overwhelming. Ellery I and Ellery II, whom I have called X, were different people. The question then arises: who was X?

Here it must be said frankly that we move in the fields of conjecture. As was said at the beginning we know little about the background of the Queens, except that that was not their name. Ellery was a native of New York City, but was his father born in the United States? The fact that Richard Queen was a student in Germany suggests a European origin, and the feeling is strong in my mind that the 'Queens' may have been a Jewish family from Germany or further East, who left their country at the time of one of the late nineteenth-century pogroms. Judge Macklin, who sponsored Richard Queen's early career in the New York police, could perhaps have filled in some of the gaps (and have told us what happened to Richard's wife), but the Judge is dead long since. Where the Queens came from remains a mystery, although Ellery seems to me very much the type of the precociously clever Jewish intellectual.

My conclusion will no longer be surprising. X was the brother, almost certainly the younger brother, of Ellery Queen.

It is one matter to reach a conclusion, quite another to verify it. A visit to the United States was obviously necessary. On this visit — the same on which I saw Archie Goodwin and met the man I believe to have been the original of Philip Marlowe — I called on Frederic Dannay, who is without doubt the greatest expert on all matters connected with Ellery Queen. Mr Dannay, who lives in the pleasant New York suburb of Larchmont, listened to my ideas with courtesy, a courtesy which seemed blended with amusement. When I had finished he observed: 'Very ingenious.' Was that all he had to say? He puffed away at the pipe which he had lit as soon as we began to talk, and spoke with a care that I knew from earlier meetings to be characteristic.

'I think you underestimate, Julian, the way in which people change. You're quite right in saying that the Ellery who found Wrightsville his spiritual home wasn't the cocky young fellow of the early books. He'd grown up, matured, become a real human being. I don't see any need to suggest that he was physically a different person.'

'What about the pince-nez? And the stick?'

'The stick was an affectation, and maybe the pince-nez were too. Perhaps he never needed them.'

'Ellery had a wife and child in Italy, you can't say

they were an affectation. And what about X's passion for baseball. When did we hear of Ellery going to a game in the early stories? And Paula Paris — '

He held up a hand and said smilingly, 'I'm not going to discuss Paula Paris. Let's just say I think your theory's clever, but not convincing. And now tell me, what's London looking like this year?'

The conversation couldn't have been called encouraging, but I was not deterred. It seemed to me that if I could discover the identity of the mysterious JJ McC, he must surely be able to say whether my ideas were true, or just moonshine. Most of his prefatory notes said at the end 'New York', and they suggested that he might have been a lawyer in close touch with the police authorities. I spent some fruitless hours looking up and talking to retired policemen who had never heard of JJ McC. I was also excited for a time by discovering that a Judge JJ McCue played a small but important part in one of the novels. Investigation showed, however, that although the Judge was a friend of the Queen family, he had certainly not written any of the prefaces. For a while I was at a standstill. Then I remembered that two of the prefaces had been written from places outside New York, and that one said simply 'Northampton'. It was in Northampton, Massachusetts, that my quest came to an end.

Northampton is a pleasant small New England town, notable chiefly as the home of famous Smith College for young women, which dominates the centre of the town. It was through a Professor of Romance Languages at Smith and a Professor Emeritus at nearby Amherst College that I discovered the identity of the elusive JJ McC — who, since he chose to use only those initials, should I think preserve his near-incognito. He had not been a lawyer, but vice-president of a large New York-based insurance company. He was a bachelor, fascinated by crime, and all his spare time had been occupied by recording the Queen cases. His connection with Northampton came through his sister, who had lived in the town for more than thirty years. It will be noticed that I have been using the past tense. JJ McC had been dead for six years.

Was that the end of the line? Not quite. I paid a call on Miss McC, who knew little of her brother's hobby (as she called it), but was very willing that I should look through his papers, which were in the attic of her pretty little white clapboard house. The attic was traditionally dusty, and I made myself very dirty in searching among dozens of cardboard files which were mostly concerned with insurance affairs, but the search was not without reward.

Among notes of several cases clearly related to Ellery I found a fragment of a different kind. The central character is named only as Dan, but I have no doubt that he was Ellery's younger brother, Dan Queen. He was a student at Amherst College, which in the eyes of its alumni is in no way inferior to Harvard. I had realized some time earlier that since Ellery went to Harvard, the family would be very likely to have sent another brother elsewhere. Even to call the fragment a story is an exaggeration, for it is hardly more than an anecdote. It is set in the mid-twenties, and even in JJ McC's rather 'period' prose there are distinct similarities to the young Ellery in Dan. He shows the germ of an intellectual acuity which unmistakably belongs to the brother of Ellery Queen.

Here, then, is the sketch that JJ McC called *Dan and the Fair Sabrina*:

'A glorious day,' said young Daniel, as he strode across the greensward from Williston Hall to South Pleasant, bobbing his head at the squirrels who scampered up trees as he approached. 'A fabulous first of May,' he cried as he passed the President's House and College Hall. 'A May day for fair Sabrina,' he remarked as he came to the four-ways junction of South and North Pleasant, Amity and Main. 'Who is Sabrina, what is she?' he almost carolled as he crossed the road, and as he went down North Pleasant he could not refrain from singing the last verse of the Sabrina song:

Sabrina fair, Sabrina dear,
We raise to thee our hearty cheer.
Come fellows all, and give a toast
To her we love, and love the most.

And who was the Sabrina about whom young Dan sang so lustily? Why, nobody less than the class goddess of Amherst College, a bronze statue presented to the College in 1857 by Governor Joel Hayden of Massachusetts. Sabrina was four-and-a-half feet high and weighed three hundred and fifty pounds, and at once attracted the attention of students, chiefly because although a little chaste drapery covered her middle regions, her upper part was entirely unclothed. Successive generations of students dressed her in women's clothes, whitewashed her, painted her black. As students became more obsessed with her, she was carried off from her place in a flower bed near North College Dormitory, and was missing for a week. Her true celebrity began, however, when she was adopted as a Goddess by the Class of '90, who stole her in their freshman year. She was then stolen back by the Class of '91 so that she crowned the '91 Class Banquet. Thereafter her career was extraordinary. Pitched battles were fought for Sabrina, she was hidden in a blacksmith's shop, among the wharves of Boston docks, in the Connecticut river. In 1894 a warrant was issued for the arrest of a student who had stolen the Goddess. He fled to Europe, and in the following year Pinkerton men searched unsuccessfully for the missing Sabrina. In 1909, by a daring stroke, she was brought to the scene of a College basketball game in a magnificent seven-seater Royal Tourist, and driven round the field.

In the end these and similar activities, with the frequent fights that ensued, tried the authorities' patience too far. An ordinance went out that no guns or heavy cudgels were to be used for Sabrina's protection, and that she could not be placed in storage vaults or lodged, as she had once been, in jail. Worst of all, she had to be shown on campus when the authorities directed, at least once in the football and once in the baseball season. The practice of creating Sabrina replicas was strictly forbidden.

For years now the edicts had been obeyed, and the worship of Sabrina had lost much of its savour. It was Dan's intention to revive true adoration of the Goddess by the creation of a copy, which would be kept in his room. There at a weekly ceremony accompanied by the quaffing of many pints of beer, and of course with the door locked and bolted against intruders, Sabrina would again be praised in song. Is not a copy a replica? Not at all, Dan planned to reply if faced by an indignant Dean. A replica should by dictionary definition be the same size as the original, carried out in the same materials, the work of the same artist. His Sabrina would be less than half the original in height, had been created in terracotta instead of bronze, and of course was not the work of the artist who had created the original more than sixty years ago. Was it possible that the Dean might remain unconvinced? Dan, known to be the finest debater of his year, was prepared to debate the matter endlessly, if necessary by appeal to the President himself.

And today, on this fine May day, he was going to collect his Sabrina. He had seen the completed figure earlier that morning, not much more than an hour ago, in the studio of Ben Hayward, who had created the piece of statuary for him. Half-a-dozen young men had gathered round in admiration, all of them Dan's friends and classmates except Ben — Paul Green who was English, Barry Newsome, Tom Leland, Billy Williams. There Sabrina sat, among much bigger works of the same dull ochre complexion. Ben specialized in terracotta work, most of it very large, and he was engaged at present in representing the Labours of Hercules in terracotta. The more-than-lifesize figures stood around like primitive statues in the great barn where the sculptor worked, the Stymphalian birds with their long curved beaks, Cerberus looking like a triple-headed oversize Hound of the Baskervilles, the Nemean lion, the furious horses of Diomedes, and — a work only just finished — the Lernean Hydra with its new heads visibly sprouting as Hercules cut the old ones off. Hercules bore a certain resemblance to the sculptor, who was a large, muscular man.

Each piece stood on a plinth which bore Ben's name and the date of its completion. It was his boast that he executed each work in two weeks, and intended to show these Herculean labours to the world when the set was complete. Dan could not make up his mind whether Ben was a genius or a megalomaniac. Perhaps both.

In any event, he had carried out the Sabrina commission quickly, and now Dan was on his way to collect the Goddess. He carried with him, for the purpose of concealing her, a large canvas bag.

Tom Leland stood against the studio door, his face gloomy. He opened it to call out as Dan approached, 'Here he is,' and then stood aside. Dan went in.

Paul, Barry and Billy Williams confronted him, and one look at their woebegone faces showed him that something was wrong. As he entered, Ben came in from his workshop at the back. 'I can't find —' he began, and then broke off when he saw Dan.

'Can't find what?' Dan looked round. The Herculean series overpowered everything else in the studio, but there were a dozen smaller pieces of work around, mostly heads in stone and terracotta. But no Sabrina. Where was she?

Paul Green anticipated his question by saying, in his clipped English tones, 'She's gone.'

'*Gone,*' Dan said unbelievingly. He put down the canvas bag. 'Where to?'

'One of *them* must have taken her,' Barry said. *They* were the class of the following year, notorious enemies.

'But that's impossible. How would they know about it?'

'It is impossible,' Barry agreed. He was a solemn young man, who wore horn-rimmed spectacles. 'You'll say so when you hear.'

'Dan found that missing money last semester,' Tom Leland said.

'And he solved the business about how the Dean's wife lost her bracelet in the clam chowder.' That was Barry again. It was true that Dan had a reputation on campus as a solver of mysteries, so that the 'Amherst Student' had run a piece about the student they called 'our local Sherlock'. He asked again what happened.

'Nothing happened,' Barry said, and then gave up. 'Ben, you tell it.'

The sculptor flung himself down on an old sofa, and looked at Dan with what might have been amusement. 'Nothing's just about right. When you left around an hour ago your Sabrina was standing on a table near the Hydra, right? About five minutes later I said to the boys I wanted to incise the inscription for the Hydra — I'd just finished it this morning. They helped me take the Hydra off its plinth, then I took the plinth into the workshop next door, right?' Dan nodded. The students often came to the studio, and Paul was taking a course with the sculptor in use of the chisel, especially in lettering. 'Clear out, I said, I'm going to work. So they cleared out —'

'But only across the road, to the College Drugstore,' said Tom.

'We ordered ice cream sodas.' That was Paul.

'And sat by the window,' owlish Barry added. 'I was in a seat where I could see straight across to the studio. So could Tom. And we were watching the door, waiting for Ben to give us a call when he'd finished, 'cause we wanted to be there when you came to collect Sabrina.'

Tom: 'Nobody came in. Nobody went out.'

Ben took up the tale again. 'There's a back door from the workshop to an alley off North Pleasant,

BEN HAYWARD
THE LERNEAN HYDRA
FINISHED 1·5·26

but to get in that way anybody would have had to pass me. Nobody passed me. The door to the studio was open, and although I wasn't looking specially I'd have noticed if somebody had come in. Anyway, the boys were out there watching the front, and there's no other entrance, just the front and the one through the workshop. I finished the inscription and brought the plinth back in.' He gestured towards the plinth which said in capitals: *Ben Hayward, The Lernean Hydra. Finished 1/5/26.* 'I whistled the boys to come, and we put the Hydra back. And then one of them, I think it was Barry, said "Hey, where's Sabrina?"'

'She'd gone,' said Tom Leland. 'Vanished. And nobody had been in or out.'

'Like I said, it's impossible,' Barry observed gravely. 'More than two-feet high and the same across. Impossible, but it happened.'

They were all looking at Dan, and he lifted his head like a hound getting the scent, and stared back at them. Then he began to prowl round the studio, walking with a hunter's delicacy. He checked the windows, which were fastened and had patent locks on the inside. He took the ladder standing in a corner, planted it so that he could reach the skylight, and went up the ladder.

The others watched. Barry said, 'We'd have seen anybody who climbed up on the roof.'

Dan merely smiled. He repeated the process in the workshop, with the same result. Then he went round both rooms, searching Ben's large tool box, opening an ottoman the sculptor kept in the workshop, moving pieces of unfinished work standing in corners, stepping always with the same delicate tread. And still the others watched, his friends with what seemed slight uneasiness, Ben Hayward with amusement. The search was not lengthy, for there were few places in which an article the size of Dan's Sabrina could have been hidden. Then Dan sank to his knees and examined the inscription below the Lernean Hydra.

'You did this quickly, Ben, even for you.'

The sculptor nodded. 'I began it a day or two ago, knew I should finish it today.'

'And you finished the inscription this morning? In person?'

'Of course.' Ben looked at the inscription, then began to laugh. 'Oh dear, oh my,' he said.

Dan turned to his friends. 'I know the impulse to take Dan down a peg must be strong, but you'll have to be more careful next time. Come along now, repeat what you kindly did for Ben earlier today. Take the Hydra off its plinth.'

His tone was so masterful that, sheepishly, they obeyed. With the figure removed Sabrina was revealed, nestling comfortably in the place within the plinth hollowed out to contain her. Dan picked up Sabrina, kissed the Goddess chastely on the cheek, and put her down.

'It was just a test,' Barry said. 'We were kidding, that's all.'

Tom Leland asked, 'How did you know? What did we do wrong?'

Dan spoke in tones that sounded uncomfortably like those of a lecturer. 'First, you presented me with an impossibility. If the facts were as you and Ben stated, why then, nobody could have got into the studio, so that Sabrina must still be here. Then it struck me that the scene bore signs of being carefully set, that it was a little strange you should be in the window seat of the College Drugstore, conveniently placed to see the studio. So I suspected a trick. When I looked at the inscription, and Ben said he'd done it, I knew I was right.'

Barry said, 'How's that? I don't understand.'

'The plinth had been prepared specially, it's just a mock-up, not the one that will be used eventually. As soon as I saw the inscription I knew Paul, not Ben, had done the lettering. You just went along with the joke, Ben, without taking any part in it.'

Ben nodded. Barry said, 'I still don't understand.'

'Today's the first of May, and Paul did the date English style, 1/5/26. If it had been Ben or any American who incised that date he would have made it 5/1/26. That's when I knew for certain I was being kidded, and also knew where you must have hidden Sabrina. After all, there was nowhere else she could be.'

Paul groaned. Tom Leland said, 'Perfidious Albion, she always lets you down.' Ben suggested that they should toast the genius in beer. Dan agreed, on condition that the toast was Sabrina. And in this manner the Goddess was worshipped once more.

* * *

There is the manuscript. I should add that when I sent it to Fred Dannay he replied: 'I don't think I should say anything, except that, although the trick about the date is a very old one, unlike Queen Victoria I was amused. Otherwise, no comment.' From which it must be assumed that the greatest living expert on the subject was not impressed. I am not dismayed, however, and still hope to discover further evidence that shows conclusively the existence of the two Ellery Queens.

About Maigret and the Stolen Papers

FROM THE WINDOW OF THE FLAT IN THE Boulevard Richard-Lenoir Maigret could see that it was a fine morning. There had been a week of gusty, rainy weather, the kind you must expect in early March as everybody said, but now it was spring. He could see it all from the window, the sun shining, girls wearing new dresses, young men in light-coloured suits. He would have liked to be out there, among it all, catching on his nostrils the early morning smell of Paris that would still be lingering in the air, coffee and hot croissants, with just a hint of rum. Meanwhile — he looked at the paper in front of him, the sheets in the wastepaper basket, and sighed.

His wife called: 'What is it?'

A good smell came from the kitchen. 'What's for lunch?'

'Morue à la crème.'

One of his favourites! But still, he sighed again. Madame Maigret appeared in the doorway. She was wearing a cotton housecoat he particularly liked, one printed all over with little flowers. 'What's the matter?'

'It's that devil Simenon. He's got things all wrong again.'

'What is it this time? Not the bowler hat?'

Simenon had spotted a bowler hat in Maigret's office cupboard, and had put it in several stories. It was an old hat, and for years now he had been wearing a trilby like other people.

'Not the hat this time, it's just . . .' Just that the portrait was not quite right, not Maigret. Or not the whole of Maigret. 'He saw me at the office, followed me about on cases, but how much does he know about me after all? I'm trying to put down something that will help him, details about my life,

It's not so easy.' He hated paper work. The only job he ever shirked was writing up reports. 'Listen to this.'

'Fifteen minutes. Then I must go back to the kitchen.'

'It won't take long. I have jotted things down very briefly. Born in central France, not far from Moulins. I shan't give the date, why should readers know everything about me? Grandfather a tenant farmer, and farming goes back for generations. Father manager of the Saint Fiacre estate, twenty-six farms and seven and a half thousand acres. We lived in a pretty house in the château courtyard, rose-coloured brick. Other families who worked in the château lived all round the courtyard. When they spoke to my father it was cap in hand.' He had put down a pipe on the table. Now he picked it up, relighted it. 'That Florentin!'

'Who do you mean?'

'Léon Florentin. He was at school with me, the Lycée Banville in Moulins. Do you know what he said my father was? A sort of upper servant on the estate. And this was after Florentin had come crawling to me for help when his mistress was murdered. He was a rat, that Florentin. I looked up to my father. He never drank—'

'Not like his son.'

'True. Though he was not the same man after my mother's death. You know she died in pregnancy when I was eight years old, I have told you that. I was left alone with my father. He was not unkind, he was never unkind to me, but he became very silent. He was only thirty-two, a young man. Not that he seemed young to me then.'

Madame Maigret sat down at the table. Only occasionally did he talk about the past, and then he liked her to listen. 'And then the Lycée.'

'When I was twelve. I went as a boarder, but only for a few months. There I knew that wretched Florentin. My father knew I didn't like it, though I never complained. He sent me to live with my aunt—'

'The one at Nantes?'

'That's right. He died at forty-four. I was a medical student then at the Collège de Nantes, gave it up after he died. That seemed to be a time of crisis, I don't know why. I might have been a doctor, like Pardon. Instead, I became a policeman. Well, I always wanted to be a guide to the lost, and a policeman can be that as well as a doctor.' He tapped his pipe almost angrily on the table. 'The point is, what does Simenon know about all this, what does he really know about Jules Maigret? Very little. What has he ever said about my entering the police force through Inspector Jacquemain, who lived in the same little hotel as myself on the Left Bank? Or about my early years in the force? I was in uniform for seven or eight months, has he described that? Then I was in plain clothes, but I was thirty before I entered the Special Squad, the Homicide Squad. How much has he written about all that part of my life, the days when all the officials wore frock coats and top hats, and there were still horse-drawn buses? Little or nothing. Or about my first meeting with you, the invitation to your father's house—'

'You wore your father's dress suit, and kept on eating petit fours.'

'You were a plump girl in blue, with sparkling eyes.'

'Not so plump. But how could Simenon put such things down, when you have never told him about them? If you want people to know all that, you'll have to write about it yourself. But I can't stop any longer. The morue ...'

It was good sometimes to let off steam like that, although the truth was that Simenon couldn't be expected to know everything, and wasn't a bad fellow on the whole. But still, he left out too much, so that the picture was unbalanced. So much of Maigret's life was spent here in this third-floor apartment on the Boulevard Richard-Lenoir, and there was not enough about that. What about the fact that he smoked in bed sometimes, that there was a glass-fronted wardrobe beside the big double bed? What about those tedious yearly visits of Mouthon, who was married to Louise's sister, and nearly drove both Maigret and his wife crazy on

their yearly visits that lasted an interminable nine days? All that was his life, as much as the Quai des Orfèvres. Perhaps he would one day write something more than these notes, something that would describe in detail that whole early period. If he did so, however, there were a few things that he would leave out, like the slightly comic and even ridiculous affair that had begun with the telephone call from little Lapointe. . . .

It had happened years ago, in the early thirties, while he was still Chief-Inspector. On the previous night they had been to the cinema, he had been tired, and as sometimes happened had fallen asleep. Louise had not been pleased, and on the following morning he had been happy to escape to the Quai des Orfèvres. It was September, a grey heavy day, but still he was pleased to pass through those portals. Even the great central lobby, which at times seemed to him the dingiest place on earth, was comfortably familiar.

He was glad to be sitting in his old-fashioned black wooden chair at his black desk, selecting a pipe from the half-dozen in the rack, looking from the black marble clock on the mantlepiece, around the dusty shelves, and finally at the great coal-burning stove, of the kind you still see in provincial railway stations. To stoke up that great stove until the bars were red hot had always been one of the pleasures of winter. Nowadays he had a big office, a proper room for a Superintendent with its bookcase-cupboard on one wall, a desk twice the size of his old one, and the impressive-looking safe by Monard, in which he kept a bottle of Calvados for a cold day. There was a fine view of the Seine, the warmth from the big radiator beneath the window was comforting to the legs. This office was better all round, no doubt about it. But still, when he looked at the black marble clock on the mantelpiece, the single relic he had preserved from the past, it seemed to him that he had liked the old office better.

So in the old office, on that heavy September morning, he put on a shovelful of coal while he wondered what Louise would cook for him after their little disagreement. If it was something he liked, say fricandeau of veal, it would mean that he was forgiven, if it was haricot mutton, then a peacemaking token was needed. Perhaps he should take back a bunch of roses in any case . . .

At the nine o'clock meeting that day they dealt as usual with a dozen cases, and talked about twenty things unconnected with crime. Maigret's particular concern at the moment was with the proceeds of a big jewel robbery that had taken place a few weeks earlier. A jeweller in the Rue de Rivoli had been cleaned out, a professional job. There was no doubt about the thieves, they were the Duhamel brothers, Jean and Louis. The break-in showed their usual method of operation, the safe had been blown with an explosive no other gang used, an old woman opposite had seen them leaving.

Why weren't they locked up? Because the old woman failed to identify them, their houses were clean, they had provided themselves with alibis. It was a matter of waiting for them to make a move. Last week Maigret had been told by an informer that Jean and Louis were sick of being watched. They had given up hope of getting the stuff abroad quickly, and wanted to get rid of it. They were ready to sell to the Pole.

The Pole did not get his name from his nationality, for he was French, but because he was as long, thin and straight as a telegraph pole. He had an apartment in the Rue Jacob where he lived quietly with his mistress, a young woman whose beautiful but expressionless features led her to be called the Mona Lisa. Maigret had visited him there, for there were occasions when the Pole had acted as an informer himself. He abominated violence, refused to handle goods that had been obtained by beating up or injuring people, and had tipped off Maigret more than once about such cases. He did not specialize, like most fences, but would handle gold, forged francs, jewellery, almost anything except drugs. He paid very low prices, so that most thieves steered clear of him. If Jean and Louis were ready to sell to the Pole they must need money badly.

About Maigret and the Stolen Papers

On the other hand the whole story might be a fiction. Or the informer could be wrong. A watch was put on the Pole's apartment, even though he was a careful man who refused to keep anything compromising on the premises. And a man was put on to the Duhamels. Today little Lapointe was tailing them, and Torrence was watching the apartment. At ten thirty Lapointe called in.

'Chief, I think I'm on to something. I'm in a bar called Freddy's, near the Porte d'Orléans.'

'Yes.' He knew Freddy's, a workman's bar with a zinc counter, chipped and stained tables, sawdust on the floor. Dominoes and cards were played there.

'Louis Duhamel is in a café across the road.'

'Yes?'

'The Mona Lisa is with him. I am in the window, and can see them.'

'What are they doing?'

'Talking, drinking coffee.I don't think they're on to me.' Lapointe was always optimistic, but it was true that he was less familiar than older hands like Lucas and Janvier.

'Stay with them if they leave. Otherwise call me again in half an hour.'

Five minutes later Torrence rang, big noisy Torrence who was full of energy but lacked the head for anything subtle. He had seen the Mona Lisa go out, but had not thought it worth calling through specially. Otherwise he had little to report, except that a doctor had visited the Pole's apartment.

'How do you know it is his apartment?'

'I talked to the concierge. She liked me.' It was true that Torrence always got on well with concierges, hotel doorkeepers, chauffeurs. 'It is a Dr Chastel from the Rue de Tournon. The concierge thinks the Pole has a visitor who is ill.'

'Anything else?'

Torrence gave his booming laugh. 'There is a little fellow and a big one planted over the road in a café. They come out in turn and look around as though they are smelling the air. Sometimes they look at me standing in a doorway. The big fellow

might be one of us. The little one, I don't know.'

'What does he look like?'

'I couldn't tell you,' Torrence said, and laughed again. 'Do I stay here, chief?'

'I know Dr Chastel. I'll try to get hold of him. Call me again in a few minutes.'

He had met Chastel in connection with an assault case a year or two back, and had liked him. The doctor did not demur at giving the information. He had been called to see a man who was suffering from a bad attack of malaria, had prescribed quinine, and said that he should not be moved for two or three days. The man was a German, around thirty, and gave the name of Schmidt. He seemed nervous, but was certainly suffering from malaria. Chastel had seen the Pole, who was polite and calm as usual.

What had this to do with Louis Duhamel and the jewels? Very likely nothing at all. So much of police work meant sitting in an office at the end of a telephone, giving instructions and making guesses, hoping that the guesses were right. When asked about his methods, Maigret always said that he had none. He had knowledge, not method, and based himself on that knowledge. Mostly it was right, occasionally wrong.

When Torrence called back, Maigret told him to stay where he was unless the Pole went out, and then to follow him. As for the big fellow and the little one, very likely they were concerned with some other affair.

Then Lapointe's eager voice again. The Mona Lisa and Louis had moved, not once but twice. They were now in a café near the Place de la Bastille, off the Boulevard Beaumarchais. It was a big place, crowded, and Lapointe had felt it safe to go in and sit at a table. He did not think he had been spotted.

It looked as though Louis and the Mona Lisa were making sure that they were not being followed, before Louis took the woman to look at the goods. Maigret made up his mind to go out there himself. At that moment he was sick of being at the end of a telephone, even sick of his comfortable

office and the stove, which he had stoked up so that the bars were red and it was uncomfortably hot.

At the same time he was a little uneasy. Why hadn't the Pole come out himself to put a price on the stuff? What was that German doing in the apartment, and who the devil were the couple on watch in the Rue Jacob?

Outside, the air was clammy, humid. He took a cab to the Boulevard Beaumarchais. The Mona Lisa knew him, so he did not go into the café, but Lapointe was on the watch and came out.

'Still there?'

'Still there. They are on to glasses of wine now.'

'What are they doing?'

'Not much. Louis seems down in the mouth. With her you can't tell.'

'Look out.' Maigret turned away, lowered his head, put up his coat collar. He had seen the two of them at the café door. They began to walk down the street, stopped, went back and re-entered the café. On the Mona Lisa's slightly wooden features Maigret discerned the ghost of a smile. He cursed.

'What's the matter?'

'She's seen me.' Without any attempt at concealment he peered through the window. Louis was leaning against the counter looking bored. The Mona Lisa had made straight for the telephone. Maigret waved for a cab. To the startled Lapointe he said, 'Jump in.' He gave the man the Rue Jacob address.

'I don't understand. Are you leaving them?'

'The Mona Lisa was a decoy. Something's going on at the Rue Jacob, and they wanted to make sure I didn't know about it. As soon as she saw me she went back to ring the Pole and tell him the coast was clear. I wish I knew . . .'

'What, chief?'

He was worrying about the little man and the big one, but didn't say so. Instead he asked pettishly, 'Why doesn't it rain?' This humid, still atmosphere was a kind of weather Maigret particularly disliked.

When they reached the narrow Rue Jacob there was no sign of Torrence, nor of the big man. As they got out of the cab, however, a small man popped out his head from the café across the road, took a look at them, then put his head in again like a tortoise. He had long pointed moustaches and wore a bow tie. Was there something familiar about him?

Lapointe was looking up and down. 'What now?'

'The concierge.'

The Pole lived in one of those elegant, shabby

11

houses common in this quarter. The concierge was shut up in a little hutch within the courtyard. She was a woman of sixty, ugly and with a figure almost square, but still inclined to be flirtatious. 'Chief-Inspector Maigret? The other one said you'd be calling. He's gone shopping.'

'Who?'

'The Pole. When the Mona Lisa is out he often takes the shopping bag, buys the food. The other one has gone after him. A fine big man, that one.' She simpered.

'What about the visitor? The one who is ill.'

She jerked a thumb. 'Still upstairs.'

What was everybody playing at? The Pole out with a shopping basket, the Mona Lisa leading him on a wild goose chase, all of them watching somebody else. He felt hot, irritable, inclined to round the whole lot of them up and start asking questions. He told Lapointe to call the Quai des Orfèvres, find out who was free and ask them to come down. After that he was to keep an eye on the little man across the road. Maigret himself went up to the Pole's apartment and rang the bell. No reply. He rang again.

'Who is that?' The voice was weak, quavering.

'A message from the Pole. He is delayed.'

'A moment.' There was the sound of a bolt being withdrawn. The door was opened. Maigret went in.

The man was thin, sandy-haired, with a wispy moustache. He wore shirt and trousers, and was wrapped in a blanket. His teeth were chattering.

'Police. Chief-Inspector Maigret.' The man retreated in the direction of the bedroom. 'Your name is Schmidt?'

'I—what do you want?'

'To see your papers. And to know why you are here, in this flat.'

He followed the man into the bedroom. The bed was unmade, a bottle of pills beside it. An official-looking briefcase, with FS lettered on it in gold, stood open on the floor. From a jacket thrown over a chair the man took a German passport, which identified him as Friedrich Schmidt, his profession as diplomat. His name was Schmidt after all!

'All right. What are you doing here?'

'The P–Pole is a friend of mine.'

'Answer the question. Why are you here?' No reply. 'It says "Diplomat" on your passport. What is your post?'

'I was in the Congo. In Africa I picked up this cursed malaria. At present I am third secretary at the Brussels embassy.' Maigret stretched a hand towards the open briefcase. Still with chattering teeth the man said, 'I am a d–diplomat. You have no right to interrogate me. Or to come in here.'

That might be true. Perhaps it was a political matter, one not for him but for the boys in the Rue des Saussaies who were directly responsible to the Ministry of the Interior. Schmidt noticed his hesitation, and said triumphantly, 'Anyway, you wouldn't find anything.'

Maigret stared at him, then left the flat. Downstairs he asked the concierge, 'Where does the Pole go to shop?'

'In the Rue de Seine, just up the road. Sometimes he goes to a baker's nearby in the Rue de Buci.'

'Thanks.' Lapointe, who was leaning against a wall, straightened up. 'What's happened, chief?'

'The man brought something compromising with him. The Pole is getting rid of it, passing it on. Who is coming down?'

'Janvier. Nobody else is free.'

'Send him after me. Rue de Seine, that street market. And Rue de Buci.'

'Can I come too?' He sounded wistful.

'No, stay here. If the little man tries to go into the Pole's apartment, stop him.'

Then mopping his forehead, he set out after the Pole.

He had not gone very far. A couple of hundred yards away Maigret found him, among the hubbub of the Rue de Seine. He was in a horsemeat butcher's engaged in earnest discussion. Maigret remembered talking to the Pole once, when he said that horsemeat was more tender and had more flavour than the finest beef. The butcher, in a striped apron, was showing him different cuts.

Torrence was opposite, standing behind a stall,

trying to look like a shopper. Maigret asked whether the Pole had spoken to anybody in the street, or made other calls.

'He has been in a baker's in the Rue de Buci, but only for a moment. He spoke to a couple of people, didn't stop. There he is.'

'Who?'

'The big fellow I told you about.' He was a few yards away, pretending to examine some cheeses, a tough-looking fellow with cap pulled down over one eye.

The Pole made his purchase and came out of the butcher's. He was so tall that he had to stoop beneath the lintel. He must have known he was followed, and now came across to speak to Maigret.

'Good day, Chief-Inspector.' His face, like his body, seemed to be all angles. When he smiled it was as though a knife line crossed his features. In his basket could be seen the meat, a French loaf, a bundle of old newspapers. 'Strange to meet you here.' Maigret said nothing. 'I am a domesticated man, you see, I do the shopping. Sometimes I even cook. My favourite.' He patted the bag containing the horsemeat.

'Is it the favourite of your visitor, M. Schmidt?'

'Unhappily he has a touch of malaria, and can eat nothing. I must get on. I seem to have seen our friend here already.' The Pole, who was a head taller then the bulky Torrence, placed a hand on his shoulder.

They followed him through the crowd of shoppers, Maigret and Torrence and the man in the cap. In a couple of minutes they were joined by Janvier.

'What are we doing, chief?'

'Playing follow my leader,' Maigret growled. He could feel sweat inside his collar. Would it never rain?

The Pole was in no hurry. He exchanged greetings with people in the street, stopped at every stall. Was he dawdling deliberately, making fools of them? At last he arrived at the greengrocer. Fruit was displayed outside and he took an apple, bit it, nodded appreciatively at the man who stood beside him in shirtsleeves. The man put half a dozen into a paper bag. The Pole bought courgettes which went into another bag, bananas, and potatoes which were wrapped in newspaper. All of them were put into the basket by the greengrocer, and the operation was so smoothly done that although Maigret was able to see it all, he did not understand what had happened until he noticed the old newspapers in the greengrocer's hand. Then he called out.

'Just a minute, if you please.'

At these words everybody moved, as though a spring in a piece of clockwork had been released. The shirtsleeved greengrocer made for the back of his shop. Janvier went after him, the man in the cap came forward, and Torrence grappled with him. Only the Pole and Maigret stayed still.

In a few moments it was over. Janvier caught the greengrocer, who did not resist. Maigret delved into the bundle of old papers, and found a large sealed envelope. He growled at the Pole. 'You will all come to headquarters.'

'It is not a matter for you.'

Perhaps that was true. The man in the cap was shouting something about belonging to the Belgian police. But Maigret had had enough. Let them tell their stories, why not? Back in the Rue Jacob, however, he could not see Lapointe. Then the detective came out of the café with the other little man, who was even shorter than Lapointe.

'Chief, this is — '

The man drew himself up. 'I am a consulting detective. The greatest in the world.' He proffered a card which Maigret took. The name meant nothing to him.

'You will come to headquarters and explain yourself.' The Pole was saying that his guest had malaria and should not be moved. 'We'll see about

that. Give me your keys.' The Pole meekly did so. 'Lapointe, go and stay with him. Call Dr Chastel, ask if this man Schmidt can be moved, if he can call the hospital. Have him watched.'

'He is a diplomat,' the Pole said.

'I don't care what he is. The rest of you, come back with me.' Part of him was still worrying about the tiff with Madame Maigret.

Back in his office the heat of the stove had died down, which was just as well. He saw the Pole first.

'Now then, no more nonsense, and don't interrupt me. You were doing some kind of deal, disposing of papers brought to you by this man Schmidt. You were the middle man. In the usual course you would have put him in touch with his buyer, sat back and collected your cut. But he was taken ill. Perhaps there was some urgency, perhaps it was just your nervousness about keeping anything compromising in the apartment. You knew the place was being watched, so you arranged that fandango with the Mona Lisa and the Duhamels to get me out of the way while this was passed on.' The bulky envelope, still sealed, lay between them on the table.

The Pole folded his arms. 'I have nothing to say. Except that you'll find it's not your business. Why not call your colleagues in the Rue des Saussaies?'

No doubt it would come to that, but first he was determined to find out what it was all about. But he got nothing more from the Pole. He turned to the detective, and to the man in the cap, whose name was Calas. He interviewed them together.

'Let me tell you what happened as I understand it. M. Calas, your credentials have been checked. You are a member of the Belgian Judicial Police on special assignment.' To the detective he said, 'I confess, I don't understand your position — '

'I was asked by the highest State authority in Belgium to discover the whereabouts of certain missing documents.' The little man put his head on one side, which was a way he had. 'I can give no details, but they come from the Ministry of Defence. It was a simple matter for me, using my little grey cells, to discover that a woman clerk was photographing material and passing it to her lover in the German embassy, Schmidt. Do I make myself clear, M. Maigret?'

'I am a simple police official, but I think I understand. What is not clear to me is why Schmidt came to Paris.'

Calas took up the story. 'Schmidt was not a German agent, but a private operator. He sold the papers, as he had sold others, for money. The material is of interest to several European countries, and he sold to the highest bidder. When he learned that we were on his track he tried to give us the slip, came here and got in touch with the Pole. We'd have collared Schmidt when he came out. You know the Pole, of course?'

'He is an old acquaintance,' Maigret said dryly. He asked the detective, 'And why did you come to Paris? I should have thought your task was finished in Brussels.'

'True, Chief-Inspector. But me, when I am asked to undertake an investigation, I am the lion or the tiger, I do not let go.'

'I wish I could say the same. But political cases, they're not my pigeon. Now, I can't just hand these papers to you. I have first to call my colleagues in the Rue des Saussaies. Protocol must be observed. They'll deal with you, and with M. Schmidt as well. I don't know if you'll want to prosecute him.'

'I doubt it,' said Calas. 'We shall just want him out of Belgium.'

Maigret made the necessary telephone call, and then stood up to say goodbye. The little man, head to one side, a gleam of amusement in his green eyes, said: 'It has been a privilege to meet you, Chief-Inspector, and to see your methods.'

He said to the man, as to others, that he had no methods. He had simply known, by a kind of intuition, that the Mona Lisa was taking him on a wild-goose chase, just as he had understood from Schmidt's manner that the man had got rid of anything compromising he had been carrying.

Well, that was a day's work. His desk was clear. It was time to go home.

When he got outside, it was raining. He was so

pleased that he took off his hat and stood with upturned face, letting the drops fall on it. He stopped at a stall, and bought red and yellow roses.

When he got back the table was laid. Madame Maigret was sitting in a chair, reading.

He gave her the roses. She exclaimed with pleasure, and went to find a vase. What was there to eat? He sniffed. It was certainly not haricot mutton. He went out to the kitchen, looked in the oven. Chicken with tarragon, garnished with asparagus tips, one of his favourites. That nodding off in the cinema had been forgiven!

He returned to the living room, rubbing his hands. The book Madame Maigret had been reading lay on the chair. He read the title: *The Murder of Roger Ackroyd.* The face that looked up at him from the cover, apparently that of the investigating detective as the artist had imagined it, seemed vaguely familiar, like a caricature of somebody he had met. Who was Roger Ackroyd? But then Madame Maigret served the chicken with tarragon, and he forgot such idle speculations.

My friend Hercule Poirot
DIARY 1929

THE LIFE OF HERCULE POIROT

BASED ON THE NOTES OF CAPTAIN ARTHUR HASTINGS

NOTE I visited Captain Hastings at the Dorset seaside resort of Lyme Regis. He had been living there in retirement for some time, first in a service apartment and latterly at the Bideawhile Nursing Home, where I saw him. We took several walks along the sea front, the Captain in blazer and short peg-top trousers, and the warmth with which he was greeted showed that he was held locally in much affection.

The purpose of my visit was to look at the materials the Captain had gathered for a biography of his friend Hercule Poirot. Although his health remained good, he felt that completion of a biographical memoir would be beyond him, and so passed on what he had written and gathered together to me, with the request that I should make what I could of them. He had made altogether more than a hundred pages of notes and jottings. Unfortunately these notes were often repetitious, were not in narrative form, and contained remarks like: 'Angkatells — must look up further details', and 'Lord Edgware affair, Japp more fooled than I was', which are never elaborated. However, this memoir has been constructed from the notes, and contains all that Hastings wished to say about his friend. I am responsible for the form in which the notes and remarks have been put, and have added a few observations and deductions of my own, as well as a brief biography of Captain Hastings himself.

One further point should be mentioned. Captain Hastings was concerned to confirm every statement by reference to the case in which it occurred. Such references are often of interest to admirers of Hercule Poirot, but their number is so considerable as to impede the course of the narrative. Accordingly, most of them have been put at the back of the book, on page 133.

Julian Symons

ARTHUR HASTINGS WAS BORN IN 1887, educated at Eton, and before World War I worked in Lloyds. We are able to date the year of his birth from Poirot's first fully recorded case, *The Mysterious Affair at Styles,* which took place in 1917. Many years later Hastings said that the tragedy at Styles occurred in 1916, but the lapse of time had played a trick with his memory. The year must have been 1917, because Hastings had been invalided home after being wounded at the battle of the Somme. This took place between July and November, 1916, and afterwards he had spent some months at a rather depressing convalescent home. At the time of the Styles affair he was on a month's sick leave, and since it took place in July, the year must have been 1917. He was thirty years old, so that the year of his birth can be fixed precisely.

Hastings had, as he vaguely says, 'come across' Poirot in Belgium, presumably before the War. Poirot had no doubt been working on a case, and Hastings had been so much impressed by him that he also thought of becoming a detective. One doesn't think of Hastings as a conceited man, but at this time he said that he had progressed rather further than Poirot, although basing himself on the Belgian's methods. After the War Hastings, like many others, evidently felt restless. He did not go back to Lloyds, but took a part-time job as secretary to an MP, and shared rooms with Poirot at 14 Farraway Street. They had a landlady named Mrs Pearson, briefly replaced by a Mrs Murchison, and the establishment seems to have resembled that of Holmes and Watson in Baker Street.

The two men were still sharing rooms when Hastings met his future wife. His extreme susceptibility to women was often remarked by Poirot. He was particularly attracted by the shade of reddish gold called auburn, and although a highly conventional man in most ways, was drawn to women whose manners were what he might have called free and easy. The first word said by his future wife (whose hair was not auburn, but black), when he met her on the Calais express to London, was 'Hell'. More than this, she turned out to be the Dulcie part of a music-hall act called the Dulcibella Kids, her sister being Bella. It did Hastings credit that his love was quite unaffected by Dulcie's way of making a living. The only time he ever laid violent hands on Poirot was when he thought the little Belgian was about to detain Dulcie. 'With a bound I reached him and pinioned his arms to his sides.' He then told the girl to escape. Hastings called her Cinderella at their first meeting, later abbreviating this to Cinders, a name he used rather than Dulcie. After their marriage, they went out to the Argentine, where Hastings took up farming. They had four children, two boys and two girls. After his wife's death, about which we are only told that it was sudden and painless, Hastings left one of his two sons to run the ranch, and returned to England. His favourite was the youngest, Judith.

That is all we know of Hastings, except that he used his army rank of Captain to the end of his life, and that at some time he was awarded the OBE, very likely for the help he gave Poirot in a case where the Belgian was employed by the Government.

About his role as Poirot's collaborator, Hastings is inclined to be a little touchy. His notes are peppered with phrases like 'AH was there too, thank you very much' and 'HP *himself* said my deductions were helpful — not mentioned!' Several times he says that this or that statement in the published books is 'a bit thick'. It has seemed that the easiest way of making such remarks into a coherent whole (something Poirot himself would have appreciated) was to put them under various headings, beginning with the vexed question of

POIROT'S AGE

When the *New York Times* printed an obituary notice of Hercule Poirot, it suggested that he was about 120 years old. Other writers have accepted this age or something like it — Mr H R F Keating, for instance, suggested that he was 130 or more when his death was recorded in *Curtain.* Hastings

14 Farraway St.

LA POLICE BELGE

scrawled across the *New York Times* obituary: 'lot of damned rot', and added that in *Curtain* he was writing about a man, not a mummy.

The misunderstanding has arisen from one prime cause, a single reference to Poirot's retirement from the Belgian police force in 1904. It is said that he was then at least sixty years old, perhaps sixty-five. Hence, he was born in 1844 or earlier, and from this it is deduced that Poirot must have been something like 130 years old at the time of his death.

A brief examination of the facts will show the improbability of the first assumption, and the downright absurdity of the second. It seems likely that Poirot's 'retirement' from the Belgian force in 1904 should be given inverted commas. In that year he was working with Inspector Japp of Scotland Yard on the Abercrombie forgery case, and perhaps a little later on the affair of 'Baron' Altara. Five years later he and the French Commissary of Police, M. Lucien Bex, were working together in Ostend, which does not sound much like retirement. We know little of the detective's early life, except that he was a Fleming and that he was brought up and remained a Catholic, but in a rare moment of autobiography he gave a little more detail about those days:

> As a boy I was poor. There were many of us. We had to get on in the world. I entered the Police Force. I worked hard. Slowly I rose in that Force. I began to make a name for myself. I made a name for myself. I began to acquire an international reputation. At last I was due to retire. Then came the War. I was injured. I came, a sad and weary refugee, to England.

'I was due to retire. *Then came the War.*' Those are surely revealing sentences, for they show that by August, 1914, Poirot had not retired. The 'retirement' of 1904 may have been a printer's error, but more probably was diplomatic, having some connection with an important case. The police retiring age in Belgium at the time could be as early as fifty, and from his later activity it seems likely that Poirot was no older than that in 1914. His injury is a little mysterious. There is no suggestion that he was ever in the Belgian armed forces, so that the injury (which left him with an occasional limp) must have been sustained in the course of undercover work. Belgium was occupied by the Germans, but he did a lot of secret work in Britain during the War, relating to such matters as the kidnapping of the Prime Minister. This occurred very late in the War, and Poirot was employed by the British Government on the express recommendation of 'one whose word was once law in Belgium — and shall be again', which can surely refer to nobody but King Albert.

Hastings does not pretend to know the precise year and month of Poirot's birth, but in the notes he plumps for 1864. Poirot would then have been forty at the time of the 'retirement', and a little over fifty when he left his native country.

It should, of course, be possible to clear up the date positively by reference to the notes. Maddeningly enough, however, Hastings contents himself with ridiculing those who believe his friend to have been a centenarian, without giving an exact date. It seems that the nearest we can get to the birth and death dates of the great detective is to say that these should be *circa* 1864 for the birth, and a year between 1947 and 1953 for his death. Although *Curtain* was published in 1975, it is clear that the events in it refer to a time shortly after the end of World War II. These dates would make him between eighty-three and eighty-nine years old at the time of his death.

The objection will no doubt be made that a number of cases are recorded long after 1953—*Third Girl,* for example, which takes its title from that 'third girl needed to share flat' phenomenon of the sixties, *Hickory Dickory Dock*, in which it is mentioned that 'half the nurses are black nowadays', *The Clocks* and *Hallowe'en Party.* Hastings has made lengthy notes on these books, which are to the general effect that Agatha Christie has updated early cases. His remarks on *Third Girl* include: 'Remember this one well, girl's name was Eleanor not Norma. Tricky little business, took place late twenties. I was in the Argentine. HP said he'd have solved it sooner if I'd been there, very flattering. Mrs Christie, clever woman, added all that modern stuff, made it swinging sixties. Did it very well.' His notes on other late cases point out that there is little which positively identifies them as relating to the year of their publication. It is true that they refer to Poirot as an old man, but of course he was in his middle or late seventies at the outbreak of World War II.

There is nothing unusual about such updating. Maigret in his memoirs complains that Simenon mixed up dates, 'setting at the beginning of my career investigations which took place much later on, and *vice versa,* so that sometimes my detectives are described as being quite young, whereas they were really staid fathers of families at the period in question.' Mrs Christie, according to Hastings's notes, made her changes cleverly, and there are very few inconsistencies to be observed.

Another point of objection may be raised. Why were there no obituary notices in the press, if Poirot died between 1947 and 1953? I give Hastings's note in full:

> For years before his death HP had been advising HM Govt on security matters. All very delicate, spies in high places, etc. Of course his name was never mentioned in relation to Fuchs, Nunn May, etc. PM kept tabs on HP, gave positive orders when he died. No publicity. Was interviewed myself by Foreign Sec, told national security was at stake. Mum's the word, I said, message understood. Couldn't help feeling sorry for old HP though. He loved the limelight.

With that summing-up by Hastings, we move on to:

POIROT'S APPEARANCE AND TASTES

Poirot's appearance first. It is described in *The Mysterious Affair at Styles,* and for a long while after that does not vary. His height is hardly more than

five feet four inches (it would be interesting to know how he avoided the Belgian police height regulations). His head is a perfect egg shape, and is carried a little to one side. He has a bad limp, no doubt from that World War I injury. He wears patent leather shoes. He carries himself with great dignity, but is a very odd-looking little man.

The portrait is modified only by age. As time goes by, the suspicion that he dyes his hair and moustache is confirmed. He reveals to Superintendent Sugden that he uses a pomade or dye, and expresses regret that 'to restore the natural colour does somewhat impoverish the quality of the hair.' When told that there is not much grey in his hair he acknowledges frankly that 'I attend to that with a bottle,' and at one time uses a product called Revivit, 'to bring back the natural tone of the hair'. Only at the very end does he decline to a wig and false moustache.

His neatness is invariable, and he is much distressed by things like a grease spot on a suit. In the morning he wears 'a very marvellous dressing gown', which some might think garish. Perhaps because his limp has vanished, he is now often seen without a cane, but when feeling sportive or wishing to create a dandyish impression he wears a buttonhole. No speck of dust is to be seen on his suits. Pointed patent leather shoes remain his normal wear through the years, although on occasion they might be changed for button boots. On holiday he tends to wear white suede shoes, accompanied by a white suit in silk, flannel or duck, and topped by a panama hat. We learn that he occasionally smokes very tiny French cigarettes.

His breakfast habits are fairly constant. He drinks hot chocolate, with brioche or croissants. Upon rare occasions he may eat boiled eggs. It is not unknown for him to take a *tisane*, although if he drinks something in the afternoon it is more likely that he will have a pot of chocolate and sugar biscuits. He likes to lunch early, not later than one o'clock, and frequently has something simple like an omelette or trout. Dinner is 'the supreme meal of the day', and in his later years he spends some time in looking for good new restaurants of a modest kind. He favours one called Chez Ma Tante, and another in Soho named La Vieille Grandmère, where he often begins with Escargots à la Vieille Grandmère. At the end of one case, Poirot and Chief-Inspector Japp eat for lunch a mushroom omelette, blanquette de veau and then baba au rhum. 'Lead me to it,' says Japp, who generally distrusts anything but English food. In general, Poirot may be said to have appreciated good food without being a gourmet. His habit of drinking crème-de-menthe, grenadine and cassis must count against him. On the other hand, it must be said that when he bought a country cottage called Resthaven he was particularly pleased that Françoise, the wife of his gardener Victor, was a good cook. We hear of Resthaven only in one story, *The Hollow*, so Poirot cannot have lived there long.

Could he cook? He is never seen in the act of doing so, but at one time teaches an appallingly bad cook named Maureen Summerhayes to make an omelette.

And what was his financial position? He told

Hastings once that he had a little over £4,000 in the bank, plus it is true £14,000 worth of shares in something called Burma Mines, given him at the end of a case. But those were early days. In later years he obviously had no need to worry about money, and was able to pick and choose his cases. He turned down an offer of $20,000 from one man, simply because he did not like the man's face. This he was able to do in part because he never lived extravagantly, something reflected in

POIROT'S HOUSES AND STAFF

We know nothing of his family, or his background in Belgium, except what is conveyed in that one fragment of autobiography. In England he lived for a time with Hastings at 14 Farraway Street, and then moved to what is variously called Whitehouse, Whitefriar or Whitehaven Mansions, at either 203 or 228. We do not know the location, except that the postal address is W1, so that it was evidently very central. Whitehouse/friar/haven was a thirties block, and Poirot was delighted by its symmetrical and geometrical appearance. His flat was on the third floor, and we have several descriptions of it, the best being perhaps that in *Mrs McGinty's Dead:*

> A large luxury flat with impeccable chromium fittings, square armchairs, and several rectangular ornaments. There could truly be said not to be a curve in the place.

The lobby is square and white, and the living room contains 'a piece of good modern sculpture representing one cube placed on another cube and above it a geometrical arrangement of copper wire'. At one time there was a model of a foxhound on the mantelpiece, a memento of Poirot's triumph over M. Giraud, but no doubt the animal's curves proved too distressing to contemplate, and he was put in a cupboard or transferred to another room. And how many other rooms are there in this luxury flat? Apart from this living room, there is an office where the efficient Miss Lemon sits, with a desk (square, of course) for Poirot, a bedroom for the

THE HOUSE BEAUTIFUL

TIFUL

OUS INTERIORS NO.23

M. Poirot's spacious and elegant modern flat in Whitehaven Mansions W.1

23

detective and another for his man George. Bathroom and kitchen, obviously, but was there a square bath? It does not seem that Hastings ever stayed at Whitehouse/friar/haven Mansions, so there can have been no third bedroom.

George, who has 'lived exclusively with titled families' before coming to Poirot, makes breakfast but apparently no main meal, offers advice when asked for it (he takes an active part in at least two cases), and makes such nice discriminations as distinguishing between a young lady and a young person, and saying that there is 'A — gentleman waiting to see you'. George probably came to Poirot in the middle or late thirties. When last glimpsed in *Curtain,* he is living in retirement at Eastbourne.

Of Miss Felicity Lemon, Poirot's 'hideous but efficient' secretary, there is less to be said. She is old-fashioned enough to wear pince-nez, and has a sister who lived in Singapore until her husband died, and then returned to run a hostel in London, where she finds herself in need of Poirot's help. Miss Lemon is said to be like a machine, and the glimpses we have of her handling the detective's considerable correspondence justify the phrase.

The London flat in the geometrical block is Poirot's most loved and most constant residence, but he seems more than once to have attempted retirement in the country. Resthaven has already been mentioned, and at another period he came to King's Abbott, where he intended to occupy himself by growing vegetable marrows. His sojourn in both these places was short. In part no doubt this was because his life was interrupted by murder, but he impresses one as essentially urban. A great traveller, to be sure — he visited many countries, and seems to have been particularly fond of the Middle East and of train travel — but his greatest attachment was to England, and the idea he had at one time of settling down in South America somewhere near Hastings would never have done. It should be mentioned that he also briefly took a London flat in the name of O'Connor, a name that with his appearance and forms of speech must surely have been hard to sustain.

THE POLICE, AND POLITICS

The police officer most closely associated with Poirot was Inspector (later Chief-Inspector) Japp, who seems to have been a Scotland Yard detective of a very old-fashioned kind. It was natural, of course, that he should have been old-fashioned, for he worked with Poirot in 1904, if not earlier. Japp must surely have retired before World War II, and so does not appear in the later books. No doubt he was a hard-working officer, but he seems to have had no imagination and few detectival skills. Poirot saved him a dozen times from making the most appalling blunders. The fact that Japp never rose to Superintendent tells its own tale. In appearance he was a ferret-faced little fellow, and a certain meanness in him is suggested by his brusque refusal on one occasion to give a boy a penny for Guy Fawkes fireworks.

Japp seems to have felt an admiration for Poirot that is expressed often in an uneasy jocosity. His frequent question as to whether Poirot has yet induced hens to lay square eggs (Hastings was fond of the same joke) is typical of the man. His manner to Hastings was often offensively patronizing, or at least Hastings found it so, as is shown by several notes saying: 'Japp wrong again!', 'HP fooled him nicely there', and so on. Yet although he must be called a humdrum fellow, Japp just once showed a prescient touch, when he said to Poirot: 'I shouldn't wonder if you ended by detecting your own death,' a remark that curiously prefigured the truth.

Poirot had perhaps closer, although less frequent, relations with Superintendent Spence, of whom George made that remark about 'A — gentleman waiting to see you'. Bluff red-faced Spence is a country policeman, and does not mind admitting when he is baffled. He is taken to La Vieille Grandmère at the end of one case and admits that, although the food is 'a bit frenchified', it is 'not at all bad grub'. Did Poirot wince? If so, we may be sure that he did not show it.

There are some interesting sidelights on the way in which Poirot is regarded outside Britain, when he

LABOUR'S STORMY PETREL.
Do you want a
GOOD INVESTMENT?
If so, you should subscribe to our
RACING
LETTERS.
See Page 6.
THE
ILLUSTRATED
POLICE NEWS
LAW COURTS
AND WEEKLY RECORD
THE OLDEST AND BEST POLICE JOURNAL IN THE WORLD.
GREAT GLOVE FIGHTS.
ESTABLISHED 1864
READ OUR
CRICKET
NOTES.
By AN EXPERT
See Page 6.
No. 3357.
THURSDAY, NOVEMBER 28. 1936.
TWOPENCE
INSPECTOR JAPP INVESTIGATES GUY FAWKES NIGHT KILLING

meets French policemen. There is M. Caux, for instance, Commissary of Police at Cannes, who stammers: 'Not *the* Hercule Poirot?' There is M. Bex, who greatly respects the little Belgian, and M. Giraud, who says contemptuously that Poirot 'cut quite a figure in the old days', but is made to pay for such rash remarks. In almost every European country there is somebody, like Lementeuil in Switzerland, who admires Poirot and smooths his way, if any smoothing is necessary.

We can judge the extent of Poirot's fame in part by the frequency with which Government Ministers consult him. It is a great pity that we lack full details of many cases involving leading politicians, but no doubt considerations of national security prevailed. What was the name of the French General who said to Poirot: 'You have saved the honour of the French Army—you have averted much bloodshed.'? The date suggests a connection with the Stavisky case, but it is impossible to go further. We know the circumstances in which he helped when the Prime Minister was kidnapped during World War I, and also of the astonishing case in which another Prime Minister stole his own submarine plans, and about the outrageous behaviour of Lord Mayfield, who was spoken of as 'the next Prime Minister'. We appreciate the cleverness with which the detective foils the plot of the scandalmongers running *X-Ray News* when they propose to bring down the Government by revealing the share-juggling and misuse of Party funds practised by yet another Prime Minister. Yet much remains unknown. What were the 'little matters' he handled for the War Office in World

War I, what kind of work did he do for the famous chemist who worked on poison gas during that same War? Hastings does not tell us, and, indeed, very likely knew little about such matters. There remains a strong impression that, perhaps from the time of his 1904 'retirement' until his mysterious wartime injury, Poirot was engaged frequently on secret work for the British and French Governments.

We may be sure that whatever he did, Poirot was guided by a very strong feeling that it is wrong, under almost any circumstances, to take human life. This is strikingly exemplified in a case during the thirties when, in spite of acknowledging that 'the safety and happiness of the whole nation' may depend upon one man, he nevertheless insists that the man must pay the penalty for murder.

It is natural to wonder whether Poirot ever met the other great detectives discussed in this book. Since he never visited the United States, he is not likely to have encountered Philip Marlowe, Ellery Queen or Nero Wolfe. There is no indication that he knew Sherlock Holmes, and the rumours that he once met Maigret are not authenticated in any note by Hastings. But what of Miss Marple? There is a character in *The Mystery of the Blue Train* whom Poirot likes from the moment he meets her. This is Katherine Grey, who comes from St Mary Mead, and returns there at the end of the story. Did Poirot pay her a visit in later years? If so it would have been natural that he should meet St Mary Mead's most famous resident. What would they have talked about? The importance of order and method and the little grey cells, or the strange things that may happen in a pure and peaceful village? We shall never know.

POIROT'S METHODS, CONCEIT, PERSONALITY

Did Poirot have any particular method? He was always talking about the importance of neatness and order, and certainly exemplified them in his everyday life, but he varied greatly in applying them to individual cases. Hastings made dozens of notes in the attempt to show that there was a 'Poirot method', but gave up finally with the comment: 'Truth is, old HP was fifty times more clever than the rest of us, that's all.'

That seems not far from the truth, but still there are not only phrases, but certain approaches, which recur. The most famous phrase is that relating to the importance of the little grey cells. 'In the little grey cells of the brain lies the solution of every mystery'—the phrase is repeated, with variations, in every book. Those little grey cells must be used to understand the psychology of the characters, and physical clues are comparatively unimportant. 'Murder springs, nine times out of ten, out of the character and circumstances of the murdered person ... It is not the mere act of killing, it is what lies *behind* it that appeals to the expert ... I ask myself, what passes exactly in the mind of the murderer.'

One should not imagine from this, however, that Poirot adhered to Freudian views, or indeed to any school of psychoanalysis or psychology. He was, rather, an acute observer of minutiae, with a very sensitive nose for evil. He is always sensing that there is something wrong about the setting of a crime or the behaviour of one particular character. His views change at times, and may even be called contradictory. In *Five Little Pigs* he tells Carla Lemarchant, who wants children, but is concerned that they may have a hereditary taint of murder, that 'amongst everyone's ancestors there has been violence and evil,' but then in *Hallowe'en Party* he says that 'the root of a person's actions lies in his genetic make-up' so that 'a murderer of twenty-four was a murderer in potential at two years old.' He is opposed to 'too much mercy', believing that it may lead to further crimes, and prefers justice to compassion. And even his insistence that 'I do not need to bend and measure the footprints and pick up the cigarette ends' is belied by such occasions as those when he is found carefully examining the earth under a window, crawling about the floor of a summer house, or—rather unexpectedly—carrying a pair of forceps in his bag.

Among his special skills is that of a conjurer's speed of hand, arising from the fact that he was shown the tricks of the trade by a pickpocket, but his greatest expertise is shown in relation to poisons. The identification in *Dumb Witness* of phosphorus poisoning, even though the symptoms are similar to those of yellow atrophy of the liver, and the uncovering of the remarkably ingenious murder method in *The Mysterious Affair at Styles* (strychnine is precipitated in a tonic so that the last dose is lethal) are sufficient evidence of his brilliant perceptions. In all Poirot was involved in some forty cases involving poisons, ranging from such common drugs and poisons as barbitone, strychnine and arsenic, to exotic poisons like coniine and gelsemium, a mixture of alkaloids derived from yellow jasmine. Did he obtain this remarkable knowledge of poisons from the chemist with whom he worked in World War I?

In considering Poirot's alleged conceit, we must remember the modesty he showed about his knowledge of poisons, which suggests that the conceit may have been more apparent than real. In a superficial sense there is no doubt at all that he was extremely vain, both about his looks (rather surprisingly) and his reputation. Hercule Poirot, he says 'is the name of one of the great ones of the world ... The Home Secretary realizes that if he can only obtain my services, all will be successful,' and so on. There is hardly a story in which he does not proclaim his own greatness. Yet this, like his fractured English and his ignorance of idiomatic phrases, is partly assumed. He does not understand what is meant by a bee in the bonnet or one over the eight, he says that the dripping rather than the fat will be in the fire, he speaks of the red kipper being dragged across the trail. Just occasionally, though, he gives himself away, as when he says in *Peril at End House* 'the bee in the bonnet, your English phrase'. He knows the phrase, even though he may not use it correctly.

There is just one occasion when the mask drops completely. An acquaintance is bold enough to ask why he sometimes speaks good, and at other times broken, English. His reply is as near to a true answer as we are likely to get:

> It is true that I can speak the exact, the idiomatic English. But, my friend, to speak the broken English is an enormous asset. It leads people to despise you. They say — a foreigner — he can't even speak English properly. It is not my policy to terrify people — instead I invite their gentle ridicule. Also I boast!

To sum up: yes, Poirot was a vain little man, perhaps in part because of his small size. There is a comic example of this when he says, not once but twice, that Sir Montagu Corner in *Lord Edgware Dies* is 'a strange little man'. He may well have been strange, but he was four inches taller than Poirot. Yet with the vanity went the ability to turn it to good use in making suspects believe they had nothing to fear from him.

About his personality in general, it is clear that this changed considerably in his later years. Certain characteristics, like his love of neatness, dislike of draughts and preference for central heating over coal fires remain constant, but it is plain that as the years passed he settled down to a selective reading of English literature and Greek myths. In early days he shows practically no knowledge of any English writing, but later on he quotes Tennyson and Lewis Carroll, knows many nursery rhymes, connects the name Miranda with Shakespeare, mentions Lady Macbeth, recalls Maeterlinck's 'Blue Bird'. Impressed by the adjurations of his friend Dr Burton of All Souls, he learns a good deal about Greek myth. He has also undertaken a study of detective fiction, reading John Dickson Carr with more appreciation than Wilkie Collins, and producing what he calls his 'magnum opus' about crime stories. No doubt he had more leisure because he took fewer cases, but it is clear that in late years he was a lonely man, although he enjoyed occasional discussion of criminal cases with his friend Solomon Levy. He had acquaintances but no intimates, and more and more often he missed the company of 'my first friend in this country — and still the dearest friend I have', Arthur Hastings.

POIROT AND HASTINGS

It is sometimes said that Poirot showed contempt for Hastings, and even jeered at him. Hastings's notes show that Poirot's little jokes did not upset him. They reveal that he fully appreciated Poirot's superior intellect, although several notes say things like 'Of course I'd cottoned on to this' (some aspects of the Styles case) . . . 'I had an inkling of the truth but HP got there first' (*ABC Murders*) . . . 'Always knew there was something fishy about the set-up' (*Peril at End House*). But his basic feeling comes through in other notes, like: 'Was always *proud* HP chose me as his friend. I'm an ordinary chap, HP was a genius.' It is true that he was easily deceived, as by Poirot's invention of his brother Achille, but in spite or because of the fact that Hastings so often represents the views of Everyman, Poirot makes clear more than once how much he valued his friend's presence and advice, even though he sometimes puts his appreciation more vaingloriously than we would wish.

The two had, after all, gone through a good deal together. One is not accustomed to think of Poirot as being often in physical danger (although he did once suffer the risk of being poisoned by a

murderer who did not discriminate among possible victims), but still there were times when circumstances, or that constant desire of Hastings to 'be up and at them' involved them in physical risk. Hastings must have enjoyed the time when he was taken off a boat by a destroyer on express Admiralty instructions, his period as secretary to Abe Ryman, Number 2 of the Big Four, and his brief masquerade with Poirot in Paris when they became 'two loafers in dirty blue blouses'. (An odd couple they must have looked.) Above all, there was the perilous time when, gagged and bound, they faced death at the order of the mad scientist Madame Olivier. Poirot persuades her to permit him a last cigarette and places it in his mouth, when he reveals that it is a blow-pipe with a dart tipped with curare, and forces her to release them.

All sorts of questions spring to one's mind. Suppose she had denied him the cigarette? Suppose she had removed an innocent cigarette from the case — or was every one a curare-tipped dart? Or, since we never hear of these lethal cigarettes before or afterwards, was the threat a piece of bluff, were the little tubes quite innocently filled with tobacco? Such a thought, of course, never occurs to Hastings. It is this transparent honesty and decency of his that makes Poirot say, in the course of the same adventure:

> You like not that I should embrace you or display the emotion ... I will say only that in this last adventure of ours, the honours are all with you, and happy is the man who has such a friend as I have!

POIROT AND WOMEN

It might be thought that there should be a blank space under this heading, but that would be far from the truth. Poirot refers on many occasions to Hastings's weakness for auburn hair, but although the little Belgian was less susceptible than his friend, he was by no means proof against feminine charms. There are occasions when this impressionableness is assumed, as in the case when Hastings mistakenly thinks that Poirot is in love with a

woman who proves to be a murderess, but still the detective can be charmed by beauty. Was the attraction sexual? Hastings does not commit himself, but it is natural to assume that Poirot felt the passions of other men.

The first we hear of women in his life is an odd little reminiscence of his Belgian youth, when he played a game called 'If not yourself, who would you be?'. He and his friends 'wrote the answer in young ladies' albums,' albums which 'had gold edges and were bound in blue leather.' At the time he rents the flat in the name of O'Connor he tells a young woman that he once 'loved a beautiful young English girl who resembled you greatly,' and although he makes a joke of it by saying that it was all for the best since she could not cook, there is a note of sadness in his voice. It is not possible to identify the girl. She cannot have been Rosamund Darnley whom he 'admired as much as any woman he had ever met,' because she belongs to a later period.

There is one woman, however, for whom his admiration is permanent and deep. She is referred to obliquely by Hastings when he says that his friend liked women 'large and flamboyant and Russian for choice'. The woman is Vera, Countess

Rossakoff. The Countess was, we are told, 'a member of the old régime' who left Russia after the Revolution. We meet her first when she enters the Farraway Street rooms 'bringing with her a swirl of sables and hat rampant with slaughtered ospreys'. The Countess is a jewel thief, and on this occasion is outwitted by Poirot. She accepts defeat with style, and the detective admires her. Indeed, he is so enthusiastic that he trips on the stairs when leaving. 'She has the nerves of steel,' he says. She needs such nerve at their next encounter, when she is using the name of Inez Veroneau and acting as secretary to Madame Olivier, she whom Poirot threatened with the blowpipe cigarette. The Countess is mixed up with some appalling villainy, but she saves Poirot's life and Hastings's too. In return the detective arranges that her son, whom she thought dead, should be smuggled out of Russia.

There is a moment at this time when Poirot contemplates marriage to her, but he thinks better — or worse — of the idea. Many years afterwards he catches a glimpse of her on the Underground, 'a woman of full and flamboyant form; her luxuriant henna red hair crowned with a small plastron of straw to which was attached a positive platoon of brilliantly feathered little birds.' She proves to be running a night club called Hell, and in Hell Poirot and his Countess meet again. They exchange compliments, each says the other has not changed, but:

> He was fully conscious now that twenty years is twenty years. Countess Rossakoff might not uncharitably have been described as a ruin. But she was at least a spectacular ruin.

Yet he still calls this ruin 'a woman in a thousand — in a million'. The attraction she holds for him is that of the aristocrat (she is a genuine Russian countess) for the bourgeois, the large for the small, the untidily exotic for the neat and orderly. And her criminal activities, which stop short of drug trafficking, are a kind of lure too. 'You have no sense of right or wrong,' he says sadly, but he still allows himself to be embraced, so that 'lipstick and mascara ornamented his face in a fantastic medley.' He calls her Vera, and sends her red roses, perhaps a thoughtless choice of colour. Even the mechanical Miss Lemon is moved to speculate: 'I wonder ... Really — at *his* age ... Surely not ... '

We know from *Curtain* that Miss Lemon was right in that last phrase. The marriage of Hercule Poirot and Vera Countess Rossakoff never took place. That seems to have been their last meeting. But it is a pleasure to pay tribute here to the woman who was without doubt the abiding love of Hercule Poirot's life.

HOLLYWOOD BOULEVARD, LOS ANGELES
NEAR MARLOWE'S OFFICE

About the Birth of Philip Marlowe

THE DOOR WAS PEBBLED GLASS, THE PAINT was black, and the wording said '. . . *Investigations*', but the name wasn't right. When I turned the handle, though, there he was sitting behind the desk.

'You're Philip Marlowe.'

'Marlowe isn't the name on the door. You're one of those guys who never quite made reading, thought all the letters were good for was alphabet soup.' He saw that I was taken aback, laughed and put out his hand. 'Okay, let's not say yes or no about my being Marlowe, but just bat the idea around a little. What's it to you anyway?'

I told him about the bookseller who had sold me some Raymond Chandler letters that mentioned the name that was on the door, how I had checked up and discovered that he was a private detective, with a reputation for being honest and highly independent like Marlowe, that he was unmarried, had an office in the right area, was the right age. Everything I had found out suggested that he was the original of Marlowe.

He listened, and nodded occasionally. While I talked I was taking in the office and the man on the other side of the desk, checking off points in my mind. The office and the building were right: 'A reasonably shabby door at the end of a reasonably shabby corridor in the sort of building that was new about the year the all-tile bathroom became the basis of civilization.' There was a little reception room just as it said in the books, and this office had an old and threadbare bit of what had once been red carpet, the five green filing cases mentioned in the stories, an advertising calendar, three chairs that might have been walnut. There was a cigarette-scarred desk, and a brown blotter on it. Yes, it was right.

And the man behind the desk? It was a warm day, and he wore a striped shirt with short sleeves, open at the neck, dark blue pants and loafers. A seersucker jacket hung on the back of the door. Of course he was older than the Marlowe of the books, something between fifty and sixty, but still a handsome man. What did he look like? When I saw him I understood that Chandler hadn't been so far off the mark when he said that Cary Grant would have been the right screen Marlowe for looks, because this man had the kind of sophistication and style you associate with Grant. Yet behind that sophistication he was unmistakably tough, and he also looked rather world-weary and cynical. Robert Mitchum? Yes, if you can imagine a cross between Mitchum and Grant, that would be about right. None of the other screen portrayals came anywhere near his physical appearance. Bogart was too small, and the others were just wrong.

While I was looking at him, and I suppose this assessment of the way he looked went on for half a minute, he was giving me an amused Mitchum-Grantish sort of look in return.

'Made the inventory? The socks are dark blue with light blue clocks on, which they tell me is old fashioned and even a teeny bit vulgar, but what the hell, I never pretended to have much taste.' He opened a drawer of his desk. I exclaimed with delight.

'That's the "deep drawer" which contains—'

A bottle of whisky and two pony glasses appeared. I protested when I saw the bottle.

'You're supposed to drink Old Forester and Old Grandad. Chandler never said anything about Wild Turkey.'

'Tastes change. Wild Turkey is something different. Watch out for it going down.'

I drank, and had the impression that my head had been temporarily removed from my body. After that the effect was agreeable.

'And now let's lay it on the line,' he said. 'I knew Ray, he was a friend, but what is there about that to make the adrenalin active? You say you're not working for a paper? You look like an out-of-work professor who's landed somewhere he doesn't like, but that could be a front. What do you want?'

'I want to write a short biography of Marlowe. For a book. And since you're the original of Marlowe—'

'Is that so? It sounds screwy enough to be true. You want to ask me questions, where I went to school, that kind of stuff? All right, but there's two conditions. You don't mention the name on the door out there in the book, you forget it existed. I don't want kids rubbernecking around here. Or society bitches inviting me round to see whether I'm the kind of detective who just might possibly amuse their guests at dinner. Whether or not I'm Marlowe is strictly between you and me and this bottle.'

'Agreed. What's the other condition?'

He tilted his chair back and it squeaked a little. 'What's in it for me?' I was taken aback and must have shown it, for he smiled. 'Marlowe was a good guy, but he never worked for free.'

'He began at $25 a day—'

'And graduated to $40, then $50. But that's a long time ago, sweetheart, and we're talking about now.'

We engaged in some bargaining. I won't say it was hard bargaining, but it must have satisfied him because at the end of it he poured me another shot of Wild Turkey, and said he was all set. When I produced a tape recorder, however, he shook his head.

'You want me to tell you all about my exciting past, you pitch that doohickey straight out the window. I like the sound of my own voice, but not when it's played back at me with little tricksy cuts made to change the sense.'

'Is it all right if I take notes?'

'Yeah, why not? You sure you're not an English professor? You're so much like one you might be an FBI man overplaying it.'

'I told you, I'm an author, I can show you books to prove it.'

'Don't bother. Some FBI agents are nuts, but not quite as crazy as you sound. Where do you want to begin?'

'Why not at the beginning? Chandler said you were born in Santa Rosa, California, spent two years at college in Oregon, and worked as an investigator for an insurance company, and then for the district attorney of Los Angeles County. According to him you've got no living relatives, but he didn't say anything about your parents or when you were born, except that for him you'll always be thirty-eight. On the other hand, in *The Long Goodbye* he said you were forty-two. That would mean you were born in—'

He held up a well-shaped hand, manicured, ringless. 'I'm not admitting it. The background's right enough far as it goes, and I guess he didn't say anything about my parents for fear of hurting feelings. Ray was very strong about not hurting feelings, but he managed to bruise a few just the same. My father was a travelling salesman, and when I was ten he lit out and never came back. Can't blame him too much, because my mother hit the bottle hard. Good days she wouldn't be on the sauce till after I got back from school, bad ones she used it instead of breakfast. I had a sister two years younger than me—a little sister, yeah. She ran off to join a circus when she was fourteen, never had sight or sound of her since. Don't blame her either, home was a good place not to be, and that would apply to Santa Rosa as well. Around fifty miles north of San Francisco, around fifty thousand people, little town trying to be big, not far from a petrified forest and that just about says it all. Kinda place you miss if your luck's in.

'Time I went to Oregon State mother was stepping up her consumption to a quart of bourbon a day. She died in a sanatorium my second year at college, and I left the end of the semester. I'd been working nights at a greasy spoon, then when she died I thought to hell with it, what use is education anyway, how do you turn it into dollars?'

'What about those quotations from Shakespeare, and you saying Chief Wax in Bay City was "cunning, like Richelieu behind the arras", and you telling Roger Wade that Flaubert's stuff was good, and quoting from T. S. Eliot?'

He laughed, showing teeth that looked as though they were still his own. 'That was Ray, he was a real literary guy. I never said those things. I'd never heard of that Frenchman, wouldn't have known how to pronounce his name. And Eliot, I couldn't tell him from a hole in the ground. You got to understand Ray was a romantic. Some of the stuff he wrote about me was true, some he put frills on, some he just made up. Mind you, I'm admitting nothing. It's you saying I'm the original Marlowe, not me. I'm just playing along.'

'Agreed. Let's get back to your own life. You left Oregon State, and then?'

'Tried a few jobs. Worked as a freight clerk, then on an apricot ranch — Ray said he did that, but I reckon he just borrowed the idea from me. Then got a job checking out insurance claims for something called the Bargain Price Insurance. I kinda liked the work, moving around, getting mixed up with all sorts of shysters, dinges and kikes and lots of small-time grifters — '

'It's been said that you — that is Marlowe — you're anti-black, anti-Jewish, anti-Mexican. Any truth in it?'

'Not a word. Plenty of good blacks around as long as they know their place, plenty of good Jews outside motion pictures, and I got nothing against a Mex.' He lit a Camel, leaned back in the swivel chair. 'Bargain Price went bust, which is what you might expect with a name like that, and I got a job with the DA of Los Angeles County, fat guy named Wilde. Didn't like him, he didn't love me. Left after I told him he could take lessons in manners from pigs. I'd saved just about enough to rent this room and a half and get my name painted on the door. And here I am.'

'At the end of *Playback*, Chandler had you about to marry Linda Loring, and in a story he began before he died, she'd settled a million dollars on you. Any truth in that?'

He threw back his head and laughed again. His neck was as smooth and unwrinkled as that of a man half his age.

'I was never so lucky. Linda was real enough, although of course that wasn't her name and I'm not giving you any real names. We made some bedsprings creak, and if I'd played my cards right there could have been orange blossom and confetti, but I never have played my cards right when money was around, and I guess now I never will.'

'You've made some corrections to what Chandler said, and perhaps there are more on the way, so I'd like to put to you a few things he said about you.'

'Not that old corn about "Down these mean streets a man must go who is neither tarnished nor afraid," I hope? Don't give me that. I've been afraid a hundred times in my life, and as for being tarnished, if you spend your days in the gutter you don't smell like a rose, however often you wash.'

'No, I was thinking of something he wrote to a friend a month before he died. May I quote?'

'Oh yeah, do. I love that "May I quote", it's real classical.'

'"A fellow of Marlowe's type shouldn't get married, because he is a lonely man, a poor man, a dangerous man, and yet a sympathetic man, and somehow none of this goes with marriage. I think he will always have a fairly shabby office, a lonely house, a number of affairs, but no permanent connection. It seems to me that that is his destiny — possibly not the best destiny in the world, but it belongs to him. No one will ever beat him, because by his nature he is unbeatable. No one will ever make him rich, because he is destined to be poor. But somehow, I think that he would not have it otherwise."'

He had been listening carefully, nodding once or twice. 'I go along with most of that. I'm not much for poetry, but I'd say that was kind of poetic. Of course you could put it simpler, you could just say I was a loner, but it's still true. Shabby office? Just look around. Home? That's always been where I hang my hat, not much more. An apartment at the Hobart Arms on Franklin, then Bristol Apartments and that rented house on Yucca Avenue in Laurel Canyon for a while. For years I had a fourth-floor apartment, third-floor to you Britishers, in a pleasant bit of Hollywood. I got it cheap as Ray suggested because there'd been a murder in the apartment, but these days that makes it fashionable and I can't afford the rent, so I'm back at the Bristol. It isn't much, but there's a hook to hang

BOTTLED IN U.S.A
OLD
GRAND-DAD
86 PROOF
43° GL
KENTUCKY STRAIGHT
BOURBON WHISKEY
DISTILLED BY
CAMEL
CHOICE QUALITY
TURKISH & DOMESTIC
BLEND
CIGARETTES

your hat, a bed to put your girl, a table to eat your meal or solve your chess problem. Who wants more? Not Marlowe. And not me.'

'You do play chess then, as it says in the books.'

'Check. Mind you, Bobby Fischer might beat me when the wind's in the wrong direction.'

'I'd like you to tell me how much the books do correspond to the actual life of a private investigator, and something about your first meeting with Raymond Chandler.'

'My first meeting with Ray, that was a hoot. I'll keep that to the end if you don't mind. The other thing, sure, why not? But since I presume this idiot firm that's sent you out here is picking up the check—?' He raised his eyebrows.

'It is.'

'And there's the usual lack of hustle to jam the line of the best PI in LA, I'll switch on the answering service, which is something new since Ray's time, and then how would it be to go round the corner and sink our molars into something like a club sandwich?'

Around the corner there was something called the English Pub—there is something called the English Pub in every big American city—and although it had that twilight gloom of all American bars and restaurants, the drinks were cold and the service friendly. We sat opposite each other in one of those high-backed alcoves that always remind me of old church pews. He ordered Old Grandad, to remind him of Ray, he said. I had a vodka gimlet in memory of Terry Lennox in *The Long Goodbye*. Then he lit another Camel and went on talking.

'How much of me is in the stories? Hard to say exactly. Wisecracks, now, the books are full of them, and everyone says they're good. I think so too, and I reckon I've got a fairly spicy turn of phrase, but it's nowhere up to what's in the books. The way it worked out was something like this. I'd talk to Ray about a case I was working on or had just finished, he'd make notes the way you're doing now. Then he'd write it up, and boy, do I mean *up*. He'd bring me a draft, read it to me, and mostly I'd say okay, but for him it wouldn't be okay, he'd sweat away and write it again like that French guy I was supposed to know about. Is it all right now? he'd ask, and I'd say yeah but it was fine before, and then he'd thump the table and give me that owlish look he had, and say "But it's better now, it's *better*, isn't that so?". And four times in five I guess he was right.

'I'll give you a couple of cases. In *Farewell, My Lovely,* where I'm having a hard drinking session with Mrs Grayle—and I knew at the time it was about as healthy as sharing a bottle of Scotch with a cobra—she says I'm a pretty fast worker and asks if I do much of this sort of thing, and I say "Practically none. I'm a Tibetan monk, in my spare time." Now that was Ray Chandler, not me. I was too busy trying to find a way of getting to grips with that cobra for a crack like that. And then that girl I zapped on the head in *The Big Sleep,* I forget what name she was given in the book, when I asked her whether I hurt her head much, she answers "You and every other man I ever met". I asked the question all right, being a perfect gentleman, but what she said was just two words. The first was *you* and the second isn't fit for the ears of an out-of-work English professor. Ray made an improvement there all right, you could call it a transformation.'

'And the one time in five when he didn't improve what you said?'

'Yeah, let me think. At the beginning of *The Big Sleep,* when I go to see the guy he called General Sternwood, the guy asks how I like my brandy and he has me answer: "Any way at all". Now what I actually said was "In a glass unless it's Spanish, and then I drink straight from the bottle." I guess Ray thought that wasn't what he called civilized. Then he says somewhere that a room's as black as Carrie Nation's bonnet. That really got me. You're always talking about England, I said, how many Englishmen do you think have heard of Carrie Nation? What's wrong with black as an undertaker's gloves, or a nigger's belly, or a coal mine with the lights out? But he wouldn't change it. We argued the toss for days about whether an undertaker's gloves are black or white, and then damn me if he doesn't say in another book they're grey cotton. He could be pig obstinate when he felt like it.'

The sandwiches had come while we were talking, monsters that would make three of any English sandwich, and while he talked I'd been considering him again, and changing my first impression a little. There was something actorish about him, which I suppose wasn't surprising in the circumstances. He might have been an actor playing Mitchum playing Marlowe, if I make myself clear. I felt a sudden twinge of doubt about his authenticity.

'Do you carry a gun?'

He flipped aside the seersucker jacket and I saw blue-black metal. 'Have my jackets specially adapted, with a false pocket for the gun. Lighter than a shoulder holster. Easier too. All Ray's stuff about that is right. I use a Smith and Wesson now, with a shortened barrel. No silencer, too clumsy. Don't often need to use it, which is just as well. I can mostly hit a barn door at ten paces. Anything else?'

'You were going to tell me how you first met, the two of you. And I'd like to know how he came to use you as a model.'

'Right. The year would have been '36 or maybe '37, a few years after he'd been sacked from the South Basin Oil Company for being on the sauce too often. I guess he was beginning to get known as a writer — you'd know all that literary stuff better than me — but the thing was he didn't know much, relied on books. Till he met me I doubt if he'd ever been face to face with a private detective.

'One afternoon I got back to the office after a wandering daughter job, turned out she was less than a quarter mile from home, shacked up with a professional pool player. There was this guy in reception, not bad looking in a way, black wavy hair, horn rims, and a voice that was Californian all right but had some other accent at the back of it, Californian carpet English underlay, you might say. He was polite, Ray was a very polite man until something needled him, but jittery. And curious. I could see him taking the office in, much the way you did. Then he started asking about how much I got paid and what gun I used, till I told him time was money and asked him to get to the point. Which in the end he did.

'Turned out he'd been in a joint called Jody's the previous night, escorting a blonde named Louellen Singer. The dame had picked a quarrel with the boss of the place, Johnny Lacosta, who'd apparently kept pretty close company with her in the past, and this got to be a real shouting match. The girl had a nice line in name-calling which just began with saying a garbage collector who hadn't washed would smell sweeter than Johnny, and Johnny gave back as good as he got with a few phrases about her being cheaper than a flophouse whore. Well, of course our Ray had to put in his nickel, and when he gave Johnny Lacosta a broderick — '

'A what?'

'One on the jaw, or wherever's handiest. Comes from a guy named Broderick on the New York force, said to be the toughest cop ever with his fists, though I reckon they could match him in LA. Jack Dempsey used him as a bodyguard. Anyway, they get thrown out on their necks or some other part of their anatomy.

'I asked what he wanted me to do, expecting he'd ask for me to act as his bodyguard. Turned out it wasn't himself he was worried about, but Louellen. She'd been breathing flames of fury at Lacosta, and he wanted me to talk to her, maybe talk to Lacosta and tell him she didn't mean it. Ray was in the middle of writing a story, he said, and thought maybe I'd handle it better than he could, which was what you might call a masterly piece of understatement.

'"How do you know this baby?" I asked him. "She sounds a bit rich for your blood." This was before he'd really started earning, and he looked what he was, neat but not smart, nervy, a bit of a scholar — '

'Like an out of work professor?'

'You said it. Turned out he'd played around with her in the days when he was in the money with South Basin Oil, met her again, and she'd been glad to see him. I learned later on that he always had an eye for girls, redheads first, blondes next, and after that he'd take what came. Twenty-five smackers a day meant something to him then, and the fact that he was willing to spend it showed he was concerned for her. I told you he was a nice guy, romantic. There was something appealing about him. Anyway, I took the job. He gave me four days' advance pay, insisted on it.

'Louellen had an apartment in a little block of flats on Auburn Place, which believe me is not where penny ante characters like Chandler and Marlowe live. When she opened the door I saw why Ray had that wistful look when he talked about her. She was a blonde, on the tall side, with legs that seemed to go on for ever, and eyes that were the damnedest colour, first blue, then green, then grey. I'd said on the intercom that I'd come from Ray. She asked me into a living room where the furniture cost as much as I make in a good year, offered me a choice of bourbon, rye or Scotch, set me in a chair and asked what the trouble was.

'"After last night you should know. Johnny Lacosta's a bad man to tangle with. Ray thought you might need a little protection."

'"And you're it."

'"That's the idea."

'She looked me up and down, which was something I didn't mind at all. "He could have picked worse. Big handsome brutes are just what I like to be protected by. But I'm not worried about Johnny. Tell Ray not to waste his nickels and dimes."

'"It's the nickels and dimes that make the dollars." I looked around. "And dollars is what you need for this outfit."

'"Stand up" she said, and I did. She took the drink, put it on a table that looked as though it might have cried out at being treated so coarsely, and then she was in my arms, those long legs pressed against me and her tongue seeking mine. I had a close view of her eyes, and whatever colour they were, they spelled bedroom.

'When we came up for breath, I asked "So who picks it up?"

'"What?"

'"The tab for this love nest?"

'She hauled off and slapped my face. Hard. Those blue-green-grey eyes looked like the cold, cold sea. "None of your business, you tinhorn chiseller."

'We'd reached this stage in our loving relationship when the bell rang, and the look of anger in those lovely eyes was replaced by one of calculation. She took hold of a button on my jacket and said softly, "Ray's nice, I like him. Just tell him to forget me, okay?". Then she opened the door. Two men were standing there. One was tall and thin, with a nose that had a bump on the end you could have hung a raincoat on, The other was a smooth neat blond, very handsome. The young one gave me a long look, and then they were in and I was out. I knew them both by sight. The tall one was Nosy O'Donnell and his sidekick was Lefty Hansen, so-called because his left was his gun hand.

'I sat at the wheel of the Olds for a minute, trying to take it in. Remember this was the thirties, before the Organization or the Mafia or whatever you like to call it was a real power. There were bandit chiefs around, each with his own territory. Johnny Lacosta was one, Nosy O'Donnell another, they both had chains of gambling joints, and they loved each other the way a hyena loves a jackal. So why was Miss Bedroom Eyes inviting them in? It sounded to me as though that advice to Ray about forgetting her was excellent, but I doubted if he'd take it. I went to see Johnny Lacosta as he'd asked.

'I found him at Jody's, which was his chief hangout. There was a floor show, but it was really a gambling club, with blackjack, craps and a wheel. I'd never heard that the wheel was rigged or the dice loaded. Lacosta was a smooth article, black hair, regular features, neat hands and feet, and he wore a blue-black suit that shone like silk. Maybe it was silk. I'd sent in my card, and written on it "About Louellen". His office was neat like himself, the desk covered with green leather, good-looking prints on the walls. He was holding my card in his fingers when I went in.

'"I don't know you, not even by name. What do you want?"

'"Last night Louellen Singer and the man she was with, Raymond Chandler, were thrown out of your club." He nodded, watching me. "She is or has been a friend of yours. I thought you'd like to know that I left her talking to Nosy O'Donnell and Lefty Hansen."

'He showed no surprise. "Thanks for the news, but what's your interest?"

'"I'm acting for Mr Chandler."

'"Thank Mr Chandler for the information. And tell him that he has no need to worry."

'"He's not worried for himself, but for Miss Singer. He asked me to say that they didn't mean to cause trouble. If she said anything out of line she didn't mean it."

'His lips twitched in what could have been amusement. He looked down at the green leather. "Miss Singer also has nothing to fear from me. After last night I have no further interest in her."

'"Meaning to say you did have an interest? Did you set her up in that snazzy apartment?"

'His manners were perfect, he could have given lessons in etiquette. "You'll forgive me saying I feel no need to discuss my private affairs with anybody, least of all a cheap shamus."

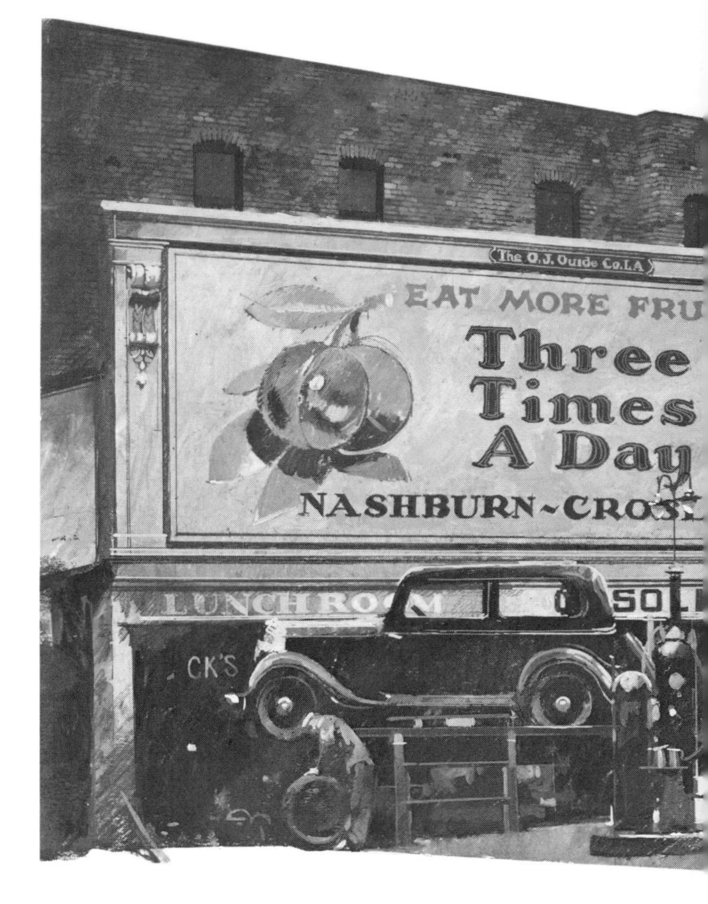

'We batted it around a little more, but I got no further. When I left, I had a shadowy idea of what might be going on. I called my client, and told him what Johnny Lacosta had said. He was writing a story, I think it was one called "Guns at Cyrano's" about a PI named Ted Malvern, and sounded abstracted. I told him to keep away from Louellen for a while, and he said she was a lovely girl but he was sorry he'd got mixed up with her, he really loved his wife. If I thought Louellen was in no trouble, he'd call me off. "Of course I wouldn't expect any money back," he said in his anxious voice.

'"I didn't say she was in no trouble. I'd like to stay on it another day or so." He said that was fine by him, and rang off.

'I bought some cold food at a deli, went back to the Hobart Arms, ate the food, put out the pieces for a chess problem, fell asleep over it, went to bed. I spent the morning at the office. Two clients came in, one who said her neighbour was writing her anonymous letters, another who believed her cat had been stolen and wanted me to find it. I was feeling gallant like Marlowe, not in it for the money. I turned them both down.

'I had to try three of O'Donnell's places before I found Lefty Hansen. When I got him I said "The girl Louellen's playing you for a sucker. She's spilled everything you and O'Donnell told her to Johnny." He asked who was talking. I ignored that, and went on "If you don't believe me try her apartment at three this afternoon. Johnny will be there." I put down the phone before he could ask who, what, why. If Miss Bedroom Eyes had taken him to bed, as I felt sure she had, he might have spilled any number of beans.

'Then I went to see Johnny Lacosta again. This time he wasn't so polite. "Trying to justify an extra day's pay, shamus? We've got nothing to talk about."

'"It's come unstuck, Johnny," I said.

'"What are you talking, about?"

'"You set it up nicely, the row here, Louellen being thrown out. Chandler was nothing, she just used him as someone to bring her along. She was your girl, not his. The idea was that she'd get in touch with O'Donnell who'd have heard of the row, say she could tell him things about your setup. Then she'd get stuff out of O'Donnell and Hansen, and report back to you. Trouble is, Louellen can't resist a man if he looks good and sounds tough. She'd have had me if I hadn't been saved by the doorbell, and she fell hard for Lefty at first sight. Five'll get you fifty she's in a clinch with him now, telling him all your secrets when she's not gnawing his ear off."

'He stared at me, his hands flat on the green leather table. Then he opened his desk, took out a little gun just right for his small hand, and put it in his pocket. He gripped my arm, so tightly it hurt, and said, "You come too, shamus. And if I find you've been lying—" He didn't complete his sentence. I certainly hoped the scene played as announced. I'd done my best to make it come true, although I hadn't quite reckoned on being present.

'Nothing more was said on the way to Auburn Place. My gun felt warm in its false pocket.

'The doorman knew Johnny, so Louellen got no warning before he rang the bell. One look at Louellen's face was enough to show that Lefty Hansen was or had been there. The bruise on her cheek was the size of a silver dollar. She said something, I don't know what, as Johnny pushed her aside and went into the living room. I followed with more caution. Nobody there. Then Lefty Hansen appeared at the bedroom door. He evidently did his beating up in the bedroom as well as his loving. He had a gun in his hand and a pair of shorts around his middle, and he was grinning as he said "'Lo, Johnny."

'That was two words too many. Johnny Lacosta drilled him three times through the pocket of the silk suit. Lefty got one off before he dropped, not a bad shot either. It got Johnny's gun hand.

'Miss Bedroom Eyes was screaming words Ray

Chandler never used in any of his books, and trying to tear pieces out of me with very long nails. I quietened her with a gentle tap on the jaw, picked up Johnny's gun in case he should be inclined to use it again, made sure that Lefty was past using his, and called the police.'

I had let my coffee get cold. 'And then?'

'And then nothing. Or not much. Lefty Hansen went underground in his lead overcoat. Johnny beat the murder rap and got justified homicide because there was no doubt about Lefty having the gun and meaning to use it. Johnny's hand mended, he made a deal with Nosy O'Donnell and they split the territory for a while. Louellen left for points east that night, reckoning that Johnny would be sore at her for going to bed with Hansen, and Nosy wouldn't love her for what she'd tried to do to him. Last I heard of her she'd shacked up with one of Capone's old mob who'd retired from the business. Me, I rang the lady who thought her cat had been stolen and said I could take the assignment, but it turned out he'd come home.'

'But what about Chandler? You said it was a hoot.'

'Oh yeah, I forgot that', he said although I was sure he hadn't. He lit up another Camel, blew a perfect smoke ring. 'The hoot was Ray's reaction when he read about the shoot out in the papers, and I told him what had happened. I thought he'd be unhappy about losing Louellen, but it was like he'd forgotten her.

'"You did that," he said "You doublecrossed them both, you took that risk. Supposing Hansen hadn't been in the apartment?"

'"It figured he would be, after my call. If not, I'd have talked my way out of it."

'"Suppose Hansen had killed Lacosta?"

'"Then I might have had to draw on him. But there wasn't much danger. It was each other they wanted, not me."

'"You took those risks for me," he said. He couldn't get over it. His eyes were moist. He gripped my hand. I said not exactly, it went with the job, but he didn't hear me. "You risked your life for twenty-five bucks a day. It's the bravest thing I ever heard." I gave a modest cough or two, didn't contradict him much. Then he smacked the office desk with the flat of his hand. "How would it be if you told me about some of your other cases and I wrote them up, changing the names, and maybe adding a little here and there. How would it be?"

'I thought he was crazy, but I didn't say so. I said to him what I said to you, "What's in it for me?" And we fixed a figure. And I began to talk. And he began to write. And that's how Marlowe was born."'

Notes to the Investigations

P. 13 'A totally inaccurate description'. The point is strikingly exemplified in 'The Lion's Mane', a story published after the events recounted above, and told by the detective in the first person. There Holmes speaks of his house as a villa, where he lived with a housekeeper. It is not easy to imagine the detective living in a villa, which in that area would certainly have been modern. The remark was no doubt a deliberate deception.

P. 14 The 'notes about a couple of matters' were 'The Blanched Soldier' and 'The Lion's Mane.' Watson did indeed make another collection. *The Case-Book of Sherlock Holmes* appeared in 1927.

P. 20 Sherlock Holmes went to the Scotland Yard, which was situated on the Thames Embankment. This was replaced by the Scotland Yard building in Victoria.

P. 22 The two cases referred to by Holmes were 'The Red-Headed League' and 'The Three Garridebs'.

P. 31 *The Murder at the Vicarage*, the first Miss Marple novel, was told by Mr Clement in the first person. The details about St Mary Mead come from several books.

P. 32 Lawrence Redding occupied the cottage in *The Murder at the Vicarage*. Many of the changes in the village are described in *The Mirror Crack'd From Side to Side* and *At Bertram's Hotel*. For Griselda's cooking etc. see *Murder at the Vicarage*.

P. 33 For Miss Marple's background, *At Bertram's Hotel, They Do It with Mirrors* and *4:50 From Paddington*. Joan West is called Miss Marple's niece in *At Bertram's Hotel*, and Raymond her great-nephew in *Sleeping Murder*. Mabel is mentioned in *The Thirteen Problems*.

P. 34 The reproduction is of the portrait of Joan West painted by a fellow student from The Slade School of Art, London.

P. 35 Ruth van Rydock mentioned Miss Marple's intention of nursing lepers in *They Do It with Mirrors*, and the Maugham plays are referred to in *The Thirteen Problems*. 'Danemead' is described, with some contradictions, in several books.

P. 36 Cherry Baker appears in *The Mirror Crack'd*, Florence in *4:50 From Paddington* and Evelyn in *Sleeping Murder*. Gladys was a victim in *A Pocket Full of Rye*. The rock garden is mentioned in *4:50 From Paddington*, the gardeners in that and in *The Mirror Crack'd*.

P. 37 For Miss Marple's appearance see *4:50 From Paddington, Murder at the Vicarage*, etc. The mimicry occurred in *A Murder is Announced*, the clothes described are in *The Thirteen Problems* and *A Body in the Library*.

P. 38 Griselda's early remarks come from *Murder at the Vicarage*. For Rose Emmott's death see *The Thirteen Problems*.

P. 40 The description of Gossington Hall, and the deaths there, come in *The Mirror Crack'd*. Mr Petherick and Dr Pender are to be found in *The Thirteen Problems*, and Miss Marple's remark about being neither shocked nor surprised from *4:50 From Paddington*. Her indignation about the film stories is in *The Mirror Crack'd*. The remark about things not said and done comes from *They Do It with Mirrors*.

P. 41 Fred Tyler is mentioned in *A Murder Is Announced*, and the bonnet story comes in *At Bertram's Hotel*. The village puzzles are in *The Thirteen Problems*, although others may be found elsewhere.

P. 43 Archie Goodwin's appearance is described by Rex Stout in John J. McAleer's *Rex Stout*. The two-foot globe is mentioned in *The Silent Speaker*. Later it increased in size. W. S. Baring-Gould's *Nero Wolfe of West Thirty-Fifth Street* says that the globe is 32⅜″ in diameter, but does not mention the conflicting sizes. The re-covering of the sofa is mentioned in *More Deaths Than One*, and the paperweight in *The Red Box*. On Archie's reading habits: he said in *The League of Frightened Men* 'I do read books, but I never yet got any real satisfaction out of one,' but knew the meaning of 'apodictical' in 'The Gun With Wings'.

Portrait of the nninteenth-century French gastronomic writer Brillat-Savarin, with Nero Wolfe's favourite foods.

P. 44 The massaranduba table is mentioned in *Too Many Women* and elsewhere, the listening panel in *The Silent Speaker* and other books. 'The best detective north of the South Pole' comes from *The Red Box*. For Wolfe's genius, often commented on, see Wolfe himself in *The League of Frightened Men*: 'I have genius or nothing.' The photograph of Wolfe gives very much the impression made by Rex Stout's remarks in McAleer. Wolfe's weight varied between 250 and an astonishing 340 lbs. Poirot's question about brownstones comes in *The Clocks*.

P. 46 'That last time with Arnold Zeck' was *Even in the Best Families*. For a detailed description of the house and office see several books, particularly Baring-Gould, McAleer and *More Deaths Than One*. 'Double-width' is Archie's phrase. The pool room is mentioned in *Murder by the Book*.

P. 48 For details about the orchid rooms see *The League of Frightened Men*, other stories, and Baring-Gould. For Wolfe's clothes, and his appearance in bed, see *The League of Frightened Men*, *The Silent Speaker*, etc. Baring-Gould mentions other breakfast dishes, including peaches and cream. Wolfe's several chairs are mentioned in *The Silent Speaker*, the argument about the typewriter in *Too Many Women*, the alarm connection in *The Silent Speaker* and elsewhere. For the button, *Even in the Best Families* and other books. For details of Wolfe's reading habits, see *Too Many Women*

P. 49 The orchid rooms were machine-gunned in *The Second Confession*, the house bombed in *A Family Affair*. Archie's remark about collecting pieces of the puzzle comes from *The Red Box*, and Wolfe's remark about not leaving home is taken from the same book, although he says similar things elsewhere. For various sausages see *Even in The Best Families*, *The Red Box* and *Too Many Cooks*. The corn cakes menu comes in *The Silent Speaker*. For the various dishes beginning with squirrel stew, see *The League of Frightened Men*, *More Deaths Than One* and *The Red Box*. The eating of a whole goose is mentioned in *The League of Frightened Men*. Archie ate that particular traditional American breakfast in *Too Many Women*. For Fritz's habits see *The League of Frightened Men*, *The Silent Speaker* and *Even in the Best Families*. For the descriptions of Saul Panzer, *The League*, *The Silent Speaker*, *Too Many Women*, etc. He was paid $30 a day in *The Silent Speaker*, $70 a day in *Champagne For One*, $80 in 'Murder Is Corny'. Marlowe came rather cheaper. For the justification of Archie's distrust of Orrie Cather, see *A Family Affair*.

P. 50 For the other free lance operators, *The League*, *Even in the Best Families*, etc. Wolfe popped Inspector Ash on the jaw in *The Silent Speaker*. The police, including Cramer, are described in many books. Cramer's initials are often given as 'L.T.', but he is called 'Fergus' in *More Deaths Than One*, a point missed by Baring-Gould. Lily Rowan, Archie's nearest thing to a permanent girl friend, makes her first appearance in *Some Buried Caesar*. Wolfe's remark about women comes from

Too Many Cooks. My own observation about the Wolfe-Goodwin household is made in *Bloody Murder*.

P. 51 'He was twenty-four years older than me'—see McAleer. There is a great deal of contradictory evidence about Archie's age, parentage and relationship to Wolfe. It is examined in detail in Baring-Gould. Archie's remark about not getting infatuated comes from *The League*. For the details of Wolfe's background, see *Over My Dead Body*, *More Deaths Than One*, *Even in the Best Families*, *The Black Mountain*. For the various theories, see Baring-Gould, and Bernard de Voto's article, 'Alias Nero Wolfe'. 'A dirty jail in Algiers' is mentioned in *A Family Affair*. The house in Egypt is mentioned in *The Red Box*, *Even in the Best Families* and elsewhere. 'I am congenitally tart and thorny'—*The Second Confession*.

P. 52 'Cocky and unlimited conceit'—*Some Buried Caesar*. Wolfe's idea of paradise is mentioned in *The Doorbell Rang*. Discrepancies about the number of people who called Wolfe by his first name occur in *Too Many Cooks*, *A Family Affair* and elsewhere. Baring-Gould says incorrectly that there was only one. For Wolfe's social views, see particularly *The Second Confession* and *More Deaths Than One*. He called himself an anarchist in *The Silent Speaker*.

P. 53 Wolfe battled with the FBI in *The Doorbell Rang*. For Archie's war service and attempt to go abroad see 'Help Wanted, Male', 'Booby Trap' and 'Not Quite Dead Enough'. For Wolfe's keen interest in Yugoslavia, 'Instead of Evidence'. The previous visit to Yugoslavia, and all the happenings mentioned in this piece, occur in *The Black Mountain*, and Carla appears first in *Over My Dead Body*.

P. 54 Charley, the cleaning man, is mentioned in *The Silent Speaker*, Wolfe's applewood cane in *A Family Affair*. It was in *Even in the Best Families* that Wolfe assumed a new personality.

Nero Wolfe's office with maps and prints on the walls, including Shakespeare and *The Coalminer*. There were eight separate lamps in this room, which would all be on at the same time.

P. 56 Archie was referring to the Yugoslav dishes cevapcici and raznici, or possibly pleskavica.

P. 57 'I've been here with Marko, hunting dragonflies.' See *Too Many Cooks*.

A rare photograph of Nero Wolfe and his childhood friend Marko in the mountains of Montenegro; reproduced here for the first time by courtesy of Archie Goodwin.

P. 62 Portrait by Thiraud of Richard and Ellery Queen. Of French origin, he found success in New York society where he was the favourite portraitist of the period.

P. 64 The quotation about 'the second and third decades of this century' comes from *The Dutch Shoe Mystery*. For more information about brownstones, see 'In Which Archie Goodwin Remembers'. Most of the details about the Queen apartment come from *The Roman Hat Mystery*, some from *The French Powder Mystery* and *The King Is Dead*.

P. 65 The apartment was invaded in *The King Is Dead*. The Inspector spoke of Ellery's brains and his own stupidity in *The French Powder Mystery*. Ellery's remark about 'Poor dad' is from *The American Gun Mystery*, 'good Polonius' from *The Chinese Orange Mystery*. Ellery at Harvard is mentioned in 'The African Traveller' and elsewhere. The quotations from Kant and others are from *The Dutch Shoe Mystery* and *The Greek Coffin Mystery*. For Ellery's height see *The Roman Hat Mystery*, for his clothes *The French Powder Mystery*. The pince-nez on their chain are mentioned in several books, as are his smoking habits and the stick. For the Duesenberg's appearance, and Ellery's coat and earflaps, see *The Finishing Stroke*. 'The Mimic Murders' is mentioned in *The Roman Hat Mystery*.

P. 66 Djuna's gastronomic creations are mentioned in *The Spanish Cape Mystery*. Ellery's drinking session is to be found in *The Four of Hearts*. The quotation about failure comes from *Cat of Many Tails*. The 'first victim' referred to relates to *Ten Days' Wonder*. Ellery is 'guided by the Inspector' in *The King Is Dead*.

P. 68 The comment about women being 'passable' comes from *Halfway House*. The sporting short stories are 'Long Shot', 'Man Bites Dog' and 'Trojan Horse'.

P. 69 The fact that Ellery was born in New York City is mentioned in *Double, Double*, Judge Macklin in *The Spanish Cape Mystery*. For the links between Frederic Dannay and the late Manfred B. Lee, and Ellery Queen, see any reference book of crime fiction.

P. 70 Judge J. J. McCue appears in *Face to Face*. 'Ellery's younger brother'. It is said in *The Finishing Stroke* that Ellery was born in 1905. but of course this contradicts the statement that he was 'Harvard Teen'. It is my view that *The Finishing Stroke* is about Dan, and that 1905 was his birth year. Sabrina: it may be necessary to assure British (although not American) readers that Amherst College exists, and bears the high reputation given to it here. The facts about Sabrina are also exactly as stated. The curious may be referred to 'Sabrina, the Class Goddess of Amherst College', a history compiled by Max Shoop, guardian of the Goddess for the Class of 1910.

P. 79 The Paris atmosphere is mentioned in *Maigret and the Spinster*, and in other stories. Madame Maigret wore the housecoat in *Maigret's Boyhood Friend*.

A view of Ile de la Cité as it would have appeared when Maigret first entered the French police. Later the weir was removed.

P. 80 For Florentin, see *Maigret's Boyhood Friend*. Dr Pardon and his wife were friends of the Maigrets, and appear in several books, including *Maigret Has Doubts*. The remark about wanting to be a guide to the lost is in *Maigret and the Headless Corpse*.

P. 81 A leaf from the Maigret family album, showing Maigret as a baby in his mother's arms, with the proud father standing by. Pages in albums of this period were almost always decorated with landscapes or architectural or floral vignettes, like those shown here. These albums were almost invariably bound in leather.

P. 82 Maigret did in fact describe the early period in detail, telling the story of his childhood, early days in the police and courting of Louise Leonard in *Maigret's Memoirs*. And Simenon later made amends for some of his omissions. See *My Friend Maigret, Maigret and the Spinster, Maigret and the Black Sheep*. Maigret fell asleep at the cinema in *Maigret and the Spinster*.

P. 96 Hastings at Eton, see *Dumb Witness*. 'Worked in Lloyds', *The Mysterious Affair at Styles*. In the same book it is mentioned that he was wounded on the Somme and invalided home. Hastings had 'come across' Poirot: *Styles*. 'Took a part-time job as secretary', *Murder on the Links*. For Mrs Pearson and the Farraway Street establishment, *The Big Four* and *Poirot's Early Cases*. For details about Cinders, *The Murder on the Links*. The OBE is mentioned in *The ABC Murders*. For HRF Keating's conjectures about Poirot's age, *Agatha Christie, First Lady of Crime*.

P. 98 Poirot's handcuffs, from his days in the Belgian police; from the Arthur Hastings collection.

P. 99 The 1904 retirement is mentioned in *Styles*, along with the cases on which he worked with Japp. He met M. Bex in *Links*. The fact that he was a Fleming is mentioned in *Poirot's Early Cases*, and his enduring Catholicism in *The Labours of Hercules*. The autobiographical fragment comes from *Three Act Tragedy*. Poirot's limp is mentioned in *Styles* and some other early books. The kidnapping of the Prime Minister is referred to in *Poirot's Early Cases*.

P.100 Poirot's appearance is mentioned in many books.

P.101 For the revelation to Superintendent Sugden, *Hercule Poirot's Christmas*. 'I attend to that with a bottle', *Hallowe'en Party*. Revivit is seen by Hastings in *The ABC Murders*. The grease spot on a new suit comes in *Poirot's Early Cases*. He uses benzine to remove a spot on his waistcoat in *Lord Edgware Dies*. The 'marvellous dressing gown', *Peril at End House*. The buttonhole is worn in *Death in the Clouds* and *Labours of Hercules*. Button boots, *Five Little Pigs*. For his varied holiday clothing, see *Evil Under the Sun*, *Murder in the Mews* and *Death on the Nile*. For the tiny cigarettes, *Death in the Clouds* and elsewhere. Breakfast habits: hot chocolate, brioche and croissants are mentioned in many books. He eats boiled eggs in *Murder on the Links*. A pot of chocolate and sugar biscuits, *One, Two, Buckle My Shoe*. Trout for lunch, *Elephants Can Remember*. Dinner is 'the supreme meal of the day', *Mrs McGinty's Dead*. Chez Ma Tante is mentioned in *Death on the Nile*, La Vieille Grandmère in *Mrs McGinty's Dead*, etc. The lunch with Japp comes in *Murder in the Mews*. Poirot and the omelette, *Cat Among the Pigeons*. Poirot's financial position, *Poirot's Early Cases*.

P.102 The offer of $20,000 came from Mr Ratchett in *Murder on the Orient Express*. His flat: it is 228 Whitehouse Mansions in *Cat Among the Pigeons*, Whitehaven in *Evil Under the Sun*, 203 Whitefriars in *Elephants*. Other descriptions of the flat: *The Labours of Hercules*, *Cat*, *One, Two, Buckle My Shoe*, etc. The sculpture, *Labours*. The foxhound, *Links*.

P.104 George had 'lived exclusively with titled families', *Mystery of the Blue Train*. George 'took an active part' in *Labours*. He distinguishes between a young lady and young person in *Third Girl*, and says 'A—gentleman' in *Mrs McGinty's Dead*. For Miss Lemon's appearance, *Hickory, Dickory Dock*, etc. Her sister comes in that book. Poirot came to King's Abbott in *The Murder of Roger Ackroyd*. For the Middle East and train travel see *Death on the Nile*, *Murder in Mesopotamia*, *Blue Train*, *Orient Express*, etc. He contemplated settling in South America in *The Big Four*. 'Took a flat in the name of O'Connor', *Poirot's Early Cases*. Japp appeared in *Styles*, and many other stories. He refused to give a penny for the guy in *Murder in the Mews*. Superintendent Spence appears in *Mrs McGinty's Dead* and some other cases.

P.105 The case featured on the front page of *Police News* and was recorded by Mrs Christie in her story *Murder in the Mews*, in which Poirot once again prevented Japp from making a fool of himself.

P.106 M. Caux appears in *Blue Train*, M. Giraud in *Links*, M. Lementeuil in *Labours*. For the French General's remarks, *Orient Express*. For the 'Prime Minister who stole his own submarine plans', *Poirot's Early Cases*, for Lord Mayfield, *Murder in the Mews*. The *X-Ray News* scandal will be found in *Labours*. The 'little matters' are mentioned in *Poirot's Early Cases*.

P.107 His work with the famous chemist is mentioned in *The Big Four*. The case in the thirties referred to was *One, Two, Buckle My Shoe*. 'In the little grey cells of the brain...' this phrase comes from *Poirot's Early Cases*, but it could be duplicated many times. The three quotations that begin 'Murder springs...' come from *Evil Under the Sun*, *Lord Edgware Dies* and *The ABC Murders*. The phrase about 'too much mercy' comes from *Hallowe'en Party*. 'I do not need to bend and measure the footprints' comes from *Five Little Pigs*, and the following instances from *Links*, *Ackroyd* and *Styles* respectively.

P.108 We are told that he was shown the tricks of the trade by a pickpocket in *Poirot's Early Cases*. Coniine and gelsemium are used in *Five Little Pigs* and *The Big Four*. The quotations exemplifying Poirot's vanity are from *Blue Train* and *Peril at End House*. His idiomatic failures are found in *Links*, *ABC Murders*, *Poirot's Early Cases* and *The Big Four*. The mask is dropped in *Three Act Tragedy*. He quotes from Tennyson in *The Hollow*, from Carroll in *The Clocks*, from a nursery rhyme in *Third Girl*. It is in *Hallowe'en Party* that he makes the Shakespearean connections, and Maeterlinck is mentioned in *Hickory, Dickory, Dock*. Dr Burton appears in *Labours*, and the magnum opus on detective stories has been completed in *Third Girl*. The discussion with his friend Solomon Levy is planned, although it doesn't take place, in *Hallowe'en Party*.

P.110 The murderer who did not discriminate is to be found in *Three Act Tragedy*. 'Be up and at them' comes from *The Big Four*, but Hastings expressed a similar wish on other occasions. All the references in this and the next paragraph are from the same work. 'Hastings mistakenly thinks...' The reference is to *Peril at End House*.

P.111 The youthful reminiscence comes from *Evil Under the Sun*. The beautiful young English girl is mentioned in *Poirot's Early Cases*, and Rosamund Darnley is a character in *Evil Under the Sun*. Hastings's remark about Countess Rossakoff is made in *Curtain*.

P.112 Poirot first tangled with Vera in *Poirot's Early Cases*, she reappeared in *The Big Four*.

P.113 The final meeting with Vera comes in *The Labours of Hercules*.

P.115 The remark about the office is in *The Little Sister*. The details of the red carpet, the filing cases and the rest are in *The Big Sleep* and other books.

P.117 For Marlowe's rates of pay see *The Big Sleep*, *The Little Sister*, *Playback*. For Chandler's account of Marlowe's early days at Santa Rosa and his later career, see *Raymond Chandler Speaking*. Marlowe's literary flights will be found in *Farewell, My Lovely* and *The Long Goodbye*.

P.118 The quotation about 'Down these mean streets' comes from Chandler's essay 'The Simple Art of Murder'. The passage beginning 'A fellow of Marlowe's type' will be found in *Raymond Chandler Speaking*.

P.120 'Black as Carrie Nation's bonnet', *The Little Sister*. For the grey cotton gloves see *Farewell, My Lovely*.

P.121 'He was beginning to get known as a writer'— some short stories had appeared in *Black Mask* and elsewhere. For Chandler's reliance on books see Frank McShane's *The Life of Raymond Chandler*.

P.128 Before Julian Symons left Los Angeles he was able to obtain a photocopy of the archive copy of the *Los Angeles Echo*, which was used as the basis for this illustration.

Bibliographies of The Great Detectives

AN ASTERISK AFTER A TITLE INDICATES A VOLUME OF SHORT STORIES

ARTHUR CONAN DOYLE
SHERLOCK HOLMES

A Study in Scarlet. London, Ward Lock, 1888; Philadelphia, Lippincott, 1890

The Sign of Four. London, Blackett, 1890; Philadelphia, Lippincott, 1893

*The Adventures of Sherlock Holmes**. London, Newnes, and New York, Harper, 1892

*The Memoirs of Sherlock Holmes**. London, Newnes, and New York, Harper, 1894

The Hound of the Baskervilles. London, Newnes, and New York, McClure, 1902

*The Return of Sherlock Holmes**. London, Newnes, and New York, McClure, 1905

The Valley of Fear. New York, Doran, 1914; London, Smith Elder, 1915

*His Last Bow: Some Reminiscences of Sherlock Holmes**. London, Murray, and New York, Doran, 1917

*The Case-Book of Sherlock Holmes**. London, Murray, and New York, Doran, 1927

AGATHA CHRISTIE
MISS MARPLE

The Murder at the Vicarage. London, Collins, and New York, Dodd Mead, 1930

*The Thirteen Problems**. London, Collins, 1932; as *The Tuesday Club Murders*, New York, Dodd Mead, 1933 selection, as *The Mystery of the Blue Geraniums and Other Tuesday Club Murders*, New York, Bantam, 1940

*The Regatta Mystery and Other Stories**. New York, Dodd Mead, 1939

The Body in the Library. London, Collins, and New York, Dodd Mead, 1942

The Moving Finger. New York, Dodd Mead, 1942; London, Collins, 1943

*The Mousetrap and Other Stories**. New York, Dell 1949; as *Three Blind Mice and Other Stories*, New York, Dodd Mead, 1950

A Murder is Announced. London, Collins, and New York, Dodd Mead, 1950

They Do It with Mirrors. London, Collins, 1952; as *Murder with Mirrors*, New York, Dodd Mead, 1952

A Pocket Full of Rye. London, Collins, 1953; New York, Dodd Mead, 1954

4:50 from Paddington. London, Collins, 1957; as *What Mrs. McGillicuddy Saw!*, New York, Dodd Mead, 1957; as *Murder She Said*, New York, Pocket Books, 1961

*The Adventures of the Christmas Pudding, and Selection of Entrées**. London, Collins, 1960

The Mirror Crack'd from Side to Side. London, Collins, 1962; as *The Mirror Crack'd*, New York, Dodd Mead, 1963

A Caribbean Mystery. London, Collins, 1964; New York, Dodd Mead, 1965

At Bertram's Hotel. London, Collins, 1965; New York, Dodd Mead, 1966

Nemesis. London, Collins, and New York, Dodd Mead, 1971

Sleeping Murder. London, Collins, and New York, Dodd Mead, 1976

*Miss Marple's Final Cases and Others**. London, Collins, 1979

HERCULE POIROT

The Mysterious Affair at Styles. London, Lane, 1920; New York, Dodd Mead, 1927

The Murder on the Links. London, Lane, and New York, Dodd Mead, 1923

*Poirot Investigates**. London, Lane, 1924; New York, Dodd Mead, 1925

The Murder of Roger Ackroyd. London, Collins, and New York, Dodd Mead, 1926

The Big Four. London, Collins, and New York, Dodd Mead, 1927

The Mystery of the Blue Train. London, Collins, and New York, Dodd Mead, 1928

Peril at End House. London, Collins, and New York, Dodd Mead, 1932

Lord Edgware Dies. London, Collins, 1933; as *Thirteen at Dinner*, New York, Dodd Mead, 1933

Murder on the Orient Express. London, Collins, 1934; as *Murder on the Calais Coach*, New York, Dodd Mead, 1934

Murder in Three Acts. New York, Dodd Mead, 1934; as *Three Act Tragedy*, London, Collins, 1935

Death in the Clouds. London, Collins, 1935; as *Death in the Air*, New York, Dodd Mead, 1935

The A.B.C. Murders. London, Collins, and New York, Dodd Mead, 1936; as *The Alphabet Murders*, New York, Pocket Books, 1966

Cards on the Table. London, Collins, 1936; New York, Dodd Mead, 1937

Murder in Mesopotamia. London, Collins, and New York, Dodd Mead, 1936

Death on the Nile. London, Collins, 1937; New York, Dodd Mead, 1938

Dumb Witness. London, Collins, 1937; as *Poirot Loses a Client*, New York, Dodd Mead, 1937

*Murder in the Mews and Other Stories**. London, Collins, 1937; as *Dead Man's Mirror and Other Stories*, New York, Dodd Mead, 1937

Appointment with Death. London, Collins, and New York, Dodd Mead, 1938

Hercule Poirot's Christmas. London, Collins, 1938; as *Murder for Christmas*, New York, Dodd Mead, 1939; as *A Holiday for Murder*, New York, Avon, 1947

*The Regatta Mystery and Other Stories**. New York, Dodd Mead, 1939

One, Two, Buckle My Shoe. London, Collins, 1940; as *The Patriotic Murders*, New York, Dodd Mead, 1941; as *An Overdose of Death*, New York, Dell, 1953

Sad Cypress. London, Collins, and New York, Dodd Mead, 1940

Evil under the Sun. London, Collins, and New York, Dodd Mead, 1941

Five Little Pigs. London, Collins, 1942; as *Murder in Retrospect*, New York, Dodd Mead, 1942

The Hollow. London, Collins, and New York, Dodd Mead, 1946; as *Murder after Hours*, New York, Dell, 1954

*The Labours of Hercules**. London, Collins, and New York, Dodd Mead, 1947

Taken at the Flood. London, Collins, 1948; as *There Is a Tide...*, New York, Dodd Mead, 1948

Mrs McGinty's Dead. London, Collins, and New York, Dodd Mead, 1952

After the Funeral. London, Collins, 1953; as *Funerals Are Fatal*, New York, Dodd Mead, 1953; as *Murder at the Gallop*, London, Fontana, 1963

Hickory, Dickory, Dock. London, Collins, 1955; as *Hickory, Dickory, Death*, New York, Dodd Mead, 1955

Dead Man's Folly. London, Collins, and New York, Dodd Mead 1956

Cat among the Pigeons. London, Collins, 1959; New York, Dodd Mead, 1960

The Clocks. London, Collins, 1963; New York, Dodd Mead, 1964

Third Girl. London, Collins, 1966; New York, Dodd Mead, 1967

Hallowe'en Party. London, Collins, and New York, Dodd Mead, 1969

Elephants Can Remember. London, Collins, and New York, Dodd Mead, 1972

*Poirot's Early Cases**. London, Collins, and New York, 1974

Curtain: Hercule Poirot's Last Case. London, Collins, and New York, Dodd Mead, 1975

REX STOUT
NERO WOLFE

Fer-de-Lance. New York, Farrar and Rinehart, 1934; London, Cassell, 1935

The League of Frightened Men. New York, Farrar and Rinehart, and London, Cassell, 1935

The Rubber Band. New York, Farrar and Rinehart, and London, Cassell, 1936; as *To Kill Again*, New York, Curl, 1960

The Red Box. New York, Farrar and Rinehart, and London, Cassell, 1937

Too Many Cooks. New York, Farrar and Rinehart, and London, Collins, 1938

Some Buried Caesar. New York, Farrar and Rinehart, and London, Collins, 1939

Over My Dead Body. New York, Farrar and Rinehart, and London, Collins, 1940

Where There's a Will. New York, Farrar and Rinehart, 1940; London, Collins, 1941

*Black Orchids**. New York, Farrar and Rinehart, 1942; London, Collins, 1943

*Not Quite Dead Enough**. New York, Farrar and Rinehart, 1944

The Silent Speaker. New York, Viking Press, 1946; London, Collins, 1947

Too Many Women. New York, Viking Press, 1947; London, Collins, 1948

And Be a Villain. New York, Viking Press, 1948; as *More Deaths Than One*, London, Collins, 1949

The Second Confession. New York, Viking Press, 1949; London, Collins, 1950

*Trouble in Triplicate**. New York, Viking Press, and London, Collins, 1949

*Three Doors to Death**. New York, Viking Press, and London, Collins, 1950

In the Best Families. New York, Viking Press, 1950; as *Even in the Best Families*, London, Collins, 1951

*Curtains for Three**. New York, Viking Press, 1950; London, Collins, 1951

Murder by the Book. New York, Viking Press, 1951; London, Collins, 1952

*Triple Jeopardy**. New York, Viking Press, 1951; London, Collins, 1952

Prisoner's Base. New York, Viking Press, 1952 ; as *Out Goes She*, London, Collins, 1953

The Golden Spiders. New York, Viking Press, 1953; London, Collins, 1954

*Three Men Out**. New York, Viking Press, 1954; London, Collins, 1955

The Black Mountain. New York, Viking Press, 1954; London, Collins, 1955

Before Midnight. New York, Viking Press, 1955; London, Collins, 1956

Might As Well Be Dead. New York, Viking Press, 1956; London, Collins, 1957

*Three Witnesses**. New York, Viking Press, and London, Collins, 1956

*Three for the Chair**. New York, Viking Press, 1957; London, Collins, 1958

If Death Ever Slept. New York, Viking Press, 1957; London, Collins, 1958

Champagne for One. New York, Viking Press, 1958; London, Collins, 1959

*And Four to Go**. New York, Viking Press, 1958; as *Crime and Again*, London, Collins, 1959

Plot It Yourself. New York, Viking Press, 1959; as *Murder in Style*, London, Collins, 1960

*Three at Wolfe's Door**. New York, Viking Press, 1960; London, Collins, 1961

Too Many Clients. New York, Viking Press, 1960; London, Collins, 1961

The Final Deduction. New York, Viking Press, 1961; London, Collins, 1962

Gambit. New York, Viking Press, 1962; London, Collins, 1963

*Homicide Trinity**. New York, Viking Press, 1962; London, Collins, 1963

The Mother Hunt. New York, Viking Press, 1963; London, Collins, 1964

*Trio for Blunt Instruments**. New York, Viking Press, 1964; London, Collins, 1965

A Right to Die. New York, Viking Press, 1964; London, Collins, 1965

The Doorbell Rang. New York, Viking Press, 1965; London, Collins, 1966

Death of a Doxy. New York, Viking Press, 1966; London, Collins, 1967

The Father Hunt. New York, Viking Press, 1968; London, Collins, 1969

Death of a Dude. New York, Viking Press, 1969; London, Collins, 1970

Please Pass the Guilt. New York, Viking Press, 1973; London, Collins, 1974

A Family Affair. New York, Viking Press, 1975; London, Collins, 1976

FRED DANNAY AND MANFRED B. LEE
ELLERY QUEEN

The Roman Hat Mystery. New York, Stokes, and London, Gollancz, 1929

The French Powder Mystery. New York, Stokes, and London, Gollancz. 1930

The Dutch Shoe Mystery. New York, Stokes, and London, Gollancz, 1931

The Greek Coffin Mystery. New York, Stokes, and London, Gollancz, 1932

The Egyptian Cross Mystery. New York, Stokes, 1932; London, Gollancz, 1933

The American Gun Mystery. New York, Stokes, and London, Gollancz, 1933; as *Death at the Rodeo*, New York, Spivak, 1951

The Siamese Twin Mystery. New York, Stokes, 1933; London, Gollancz, 1934

The Chinese Orange Mystery. New York, Stokes, and London, Gollancz, 1934

*The Adventures of Ellery Queen**. New York, Stokes, 1934; London, Gollancz, 1935

The Spanish Cape Mystery. New York, Stokes, and London, Gollancz, 1935

Halfway House. New York, Stokes, and London, Gollancz, 1936

The Door Between. New York, Stokes, and London, Gollancz, 1937

The Devil to Pay. New York, Stokes, and London, Gollancz, 1938

The Four of Hearts. New York, Stokes, 1938; London, Gollancz, 1939

The Dragon's Teeth. New York, Stokes, and London, Gollancz, 1939; as *The Virgin Heiress*, New York, Pocket Books, 1954

*The New Adventures of Ellery Queen**. New York, Stokes, and London, Gollancz, 1940; with varied contents as *More Adventures of Ellery Queen*, New York, Spivak, 1940

Calamity Town. Boston, Little Brown, and London, Gollancz, 1942

There Was an Old Woman. Boston, Little Brown, 1943; London, Gollancz, 1944; as *The Quick and the Dead*, New York, Pocket Books, 1956

The Murderer Is a Fox. Boston, Little Brown, and London, Gollancz, 1945

*The Case Book of Ellery Queen**. New York, Spivak, 1945

Ten Days' Wonder. Boston, Little Brown, and London, Gollancz, 1948

Cat of Many Tails. Boston, Little Brown, and London, Gollancz, 1949

Double, Double. Boston, Little Brown, and London, Gollancz, 1950; as *The Case of the Seven Murders*, New York, Pocket Books, 1958

The Origin of Evil. Boston, Little Brown, and London, Gollancz, 1951

The King Is Dead. Boston, Little Brown, and London, Gollancz, 1952

*Calendar of Crime**. Boston, Little Brown, and London, Gollancz, 1952

The Scarlet Letters. Boston, Little Brown, and London, Gollancz, 1953

*QBI: Queen's Bureau of Investigation**. Boston, Little Brown, 1954; London, Gollancz, 1955 *nspector Queen's Own Case*. New York, Simon and Schuster, and London, Gollancz, 1956

The Finishing Stroke. New York, Simon and Schuster, and London, Gollancz, 1958

The Player on the Other Side. New York, Random House, and London, Gollancz, 1963

And on the Eighth Day. New York, Random House, and London, Gollancz, 1964

The Fourth Side of the Triangle. New York, Random House, and London, Gollancz, 1965

*Queens Full**. New York, Random House, 1965; London, Gollancz, 1966

A Study in Terror (novelization of screenplay). New York, Lancer, 1966; as *Sherlock Holmes Versus Jack the Ripper*, London, Gollancz, 1967

Face to Face. New York, New American Library, and London, Gollancz, 1967

The House of Brass. New York, New American Library, and London, Gollancz, 1968

*QED: Queen's Experiments in Detection**. New York, New American Library, 1968; London, Gollancz, 1969

The Last Woman in His Life. Cleveland, World, and London, Gollancz, 1970

A Fine and Private Place. Cleveland, World, and London, Gollancz, 1971

GEORGES SIMENON
MAIGRET

The Death of Monsieur Gallet. New York, Covici, Friede, c.1932; London, Hurst & Blackett, 1933

The Crime of Inspector Maigret. New York, Covici, Friede, 1932; London, Hurst & Blackett, 1933

The Strange Case of Peter the Lett. New York, Covici, Friede, 1933; London, Hurst & Blackett, 1933

The Crossroad Murders. New York, Covici, Friede, 1933; London, Hurst & Blackett, 1933

The Crime at Lock 14. New York, Covici, Friede, 1934; London, Hurst & Blackett, 1934

The Shadow in the Courtyard. New York, Covici, Friede, 1934; London, Hurst & Blackett, 1934

A Face for a Clue. London, G. Routledge & Sons, 1939; New York, Harcourt, Brace & Co, 1940

A Battle of Nerves. London, G. Routledge & Sons, 1939; New York, Harcourt, Brace & Co, 1940

A Crime in Holland. London, G. Routledge & Sons, 1940; New York, Harcourt, Brace & Co, 1940

At the Gai-Moulin. London, G. Routledge & Sons, 1940; New York, Harcourt, Brace & Co, 1940

The Guingette by the Seine. London, G. Routledge & Sons, 1940; New York, Harcourt, Brace & Co, 1941

Maigret Keeps a Rendezvous. London, G. Routledge & Sons, 1940; New York, Harcourt, Brace & Co, 1941

The Flemish Shop. London, G. Routledge & Sons, 1940; New York, Harcourt, Brace & Co, 1941

The Madman of Bergerac. London, G. Routledge & Sons, 1940; New York, Harcourt, Brace & Co, 1940

Liberty Bar. London, G. Routledge & Sons, 1940; New York, Harcourt, Brace & Co, 1940

The Lock at Charenton. London, G. Routledge & Sons, 1940; New York, Harcourt, Brace & Co, 1941

Death of a Harbour Master. London, G. Routledge & Sons, 1941; New York, Harcourt, Brace & Co, 1942

Maigret Returns. London, G. Routledge & Sons, 1941; New York, Harcourt, Brace & Co, 1941

The Man from Everywhere. London, G. Routledge & Sons, 1941; New York, Harcourt, Brace & Co, 1942

To Any Lengths. London, Routledge & Kegan Paul, 1950

Maigret on Holiday. London, Routledge & Kegan Paul, 1950; as *No Vacation for Maigret,* New York, Doubleday, 1953

Maigret in Montmartre. London, Hamish Hamilton, 1954; as *Inspector Maigret and the Strangled Stripper,* New York, Doubleday, 1954

Maigret's Mistake. London, Hamish Hamilton, 1954; New York, Harcourt, Brace & World, 1964

Inspector Maigret and the Killers. New York, Doubleday, 1954; as *Maigret and the Gangsters,* London, Hamish Hamilton, 1974

Maigret and the Young Girl. London, Hamish Hamilton, 1955; as *Maigret and the Dead Girl,* New York, Doubleday, 1955

Maigret and the Burglar's Wife. London, Hamish Hamilton, 1955; as *Inspector Maigret and the Burglar's Wife,* New York, Doubleday, 1956

Maigret in New York's Underworld. New York, Doubleday, 1955

Maigret's Revolver. London, Hamish Hamilton, 1956

My Friend Maigret. London, Hamish Hamilton, 1956; as *The Methods of Maigret,* New York, Doubleday, 1957

Maigret Goes to School. London, Hamish Hamilton, 1957; as *Five Times Maigret,* New York, Harcourt, Brace & World, 1964

Maigret's Little Joke. London, Hamish Hamilton, 1957; as *None of Maigret's Business,* New York, Doubleday, 1958

Maigret's First Case. London, Hamish Hamilton, 1958

Maigret and the Old Lady. London, Hamish Hamilton, 1958

The Short Cases of Inspector Maigret. New York, Doubleday, 1959

Maigret Has Scruples. London, Hamish Hamilton, 1959; New York, Doubleday, 1960

Maigret and the Reluctant Witnesses. London, Hamish Hamilton, 1959; New York, Doubleday, 1960

Madame Maigret's Friend. London, Hamish Hamilton, 1960; as *Madame Maigret's Own Case,* New York, Doubleday, 1959

Maigret Takes a Room. London, Hamish Hamilton, 1960; as *Maigret Rents a Room,* New York, Doubleday, 1961

Maigret Afraid. London, Hamish Hamilton, 1961

Maigret in Court. London, Hamish Hamilton, 1961

Maigret's Failure. London, Hamish Hamilton, 1962

Maigret in Society. London, Hamish Hamilton, 1962

Maigret's Memoirs. London, Hamish Hamilton, 1963

Maigret and the Lazy Burglar. London, Hamish Hamilton, 1963

Maigret's Special Murder. London, Hamish Hamilton, 1964; as *Maigret's Dead Man,* New York, Doubleday, 1964

Maigret and the Saturday Caller. London, Hamish Hamilton, 1964

Maigret Loses His Temper. London, Hamish Hamilton, 1965; New York, Harcourt, Brace & Co, 1974

Maigret Sets a Trap. London, Hamish Hamilton, 1965; New York, Harcourt, Brace & Co, 1972

Maigret on the Defensive. London, Hamish Hamilton, 1966

The Patience of Maigret. London, Hamish Hamilton, 1966

Maigret and the Nahour Case. London, Hamish Hamilton, 1967

Maigret and the Headless Corpse. London, Hamish Hamilton, 1967; New York, Harcourt, Brace & Co, 1968

Maigret Has Doubts. London, Hamish Hamilton, 1968

Maigret's Pickpocket. London, Hamish Hamilton, 1968; New York, Harcourt, Brace & World, 1968

Maigret and the Minister. London, Hamish Hamilton, 1969; as *Maigret and the Calaine Report,* New York, Harcourt, Brace & World, 1969

Maigret Takes the Waters. London, Hamish Hamilton, 1969; as *Maigret in Vichy,* New York, Harcourt, Brace & Co, 1969

Maigret Hesitates. London, Hamish Hamilton, 1970; New York, Harcourt, Brace & World, 1970

Maigret's Boyhood Friend. London Hamish Hamilton, 1970; New York, Harcourt, Brace, Jovanovich, 1970

Maigret and the Killer. London, Hamish Hamilton, 1971; New York, Harcourt, Brace, Jovanovich, 1971

Maigret and the Wine Merchant. London, Hamish Hamilton, 1971; New York, Harcourt, Brace, Jovanovich, 1971

Maigret and the Madwoman. London, Hamish Hamilton, 1972; New York, Harcourt, Brace, Jovanovich, 1972

Maigret and the Flea. London, Hamish Hamilton, 1972; as *Maigret and the Informer,* New York, Harcourt, Brace, Jovanovich, 1972

Maigret and Monsieur Charles. London, Hamish Hamilton, 1973

Maigret and the Dosser. London, Hamish Hamilton, 1973; as *Maigret and the Bum,* New York, Harcourt, Brace, Jovanovich, 1973

Maigret and the Youngsters. London, Hamish Hamilton, 1974

Maigret and the Millionaires. London, Hamish Hamilton, 1974; New York, Harcourt, Brace, Jovanovich, 1974

Maigret and the Man on the Boulevard. London, Hamish Hamilton, 1975; as *Maigret and the Man on the Bench,* New York, Harcourt, Brace, Jovanovich, 1975

Maigret and the Loner. London, Hamish Hamilton, 1975; New York, Harcourt, Brace, Jovanovich, 1975

Maigret and the Ghost. London, Hamish Hamilton, 1975; as *Maigret and the Apparition,* New York, Harcourt, Brace, Jovanovich, 1976

Maigret and the Black Sheep. London, Hamish Hamilton, 1976; New York, Harcourt, Brace, Jovanovich, 1976

Complete Maigret Short Stories. London, Hamish Hamilton, 1976; as *Maigret's Christmas** New York, Harcourt, Brace, Jovanovich, 1976

Maigret and the Hotel Majestic. London, Hamish Hamilton, 1977; New York, Harcourt, Brace, Jovanovich, 1978

Maigret and the Spinster. London, Hamish Hamilton, 1977

Maigret in Exile. London, Hamish Hamilton, 1978; New York, Harcourt, Brace, Jovanovich, 1979

Maigret and the Toy Village. New York, Harcourt, Brace, Jovanovich, 1979

Maigret's Rival. London, Hamish Hamilton, 1979

RAYMOND CHANDLER
PHILIP MARLOWE

The Big Sleep. New York, Knopf, and London, Hamish Hamilton, 1939

Farewell, My Lovely. New York, Knopf, and London, Hamish Hamilton, 1940

The High Window. New York, Knopf, 1942; London, Hamish Hamilton, 1943

The Lady in the Lake. New York, Knopf, 1943; London, Hamish Hamilton, 1944

The Little Sister. London, Hamish Hamilton, and Boston, Houghton Mifflin, 1949

*The Simple Art of Murder**. Boston, Houghton Mifflin, and London, Hamish Hamilton, 1950; as *Trouble is My Business, Pick-up on Noon Street*, and *The Simple Art of Murder*, New York, Pocket Books, 3 vols., 1951–53

The Long Goodbye. London, Hamish Hamilton 1953; Boston, Houghton Mifflin, 1954

Playback. London, Hamish Hamilton, and Boston, Houghton Mifflin, 1958

*Killer in the Rain**, edited by Philip Durham. Boston, Houghton Mifflin, and London, Hamish Hamilton, 1964

*The Smell of Fear**. London, Hamish Hamilton; 1965